WINE COUNTRY COURIER

Community Buzz

Cinderella and the Rogue Ashton Prince

With Spencer Ashton's murder still unsolved, rumors are swirling all over Napa Valley like wine in a fine crystal goblet. Spencer Ashton had a way with business, but he made few friends and many enemies along the way. His scandalous love life has left behind three feuding families and bitter feelings all around. It is no surprise that the police are sniffing for suspects among some of his own offspring!

And now one of those offspring may be getting the ultimate revenge on his estranged late father. The buzz of Ashton Estate Winery is that Eli and his siblings were completely cut out of their father's will. Now Eli Ashton has been seen romancing Lara Hunter, a servant at the winery. While we hope Eli is carrying that glass slipper for his lovely lady, we wonder at his motives. Is this truly a romance, or an abandoned son's attempt to seek entrance into father's home and second family—at Cinderella's expense?

Dear Reader,

Thank you for choosing Silhouette Desire, where this month we have six fabulous novels for you to enjoy. We start things off with *Estate Affair* by Sara Orwig, the latest installment of the continuing DYNASTIES: THE ASHTONS series. In this upstairs/downstairs-themed story, the Ashtons' maid falls for an Ashton son and all sorts of scandal follows. And in Maureen Child's *Whatever Reilly Wants…*, the second title in the THREE-WAY WAGER series, a sexy marine gets an unexpected surprise when he falls for his suddenly transformed gal pal.

Susan Crosby concludes her BEHIND CLOSED DOORS series with *Secrets of Paternity*. The secret baby in this book just happens to be eighteen years old…. Hmm, there's quite the story behind that revelation. The wonderful Emilie Rose presents *Scandalous Passion,* a sultry tale of a woman desperate to get back some steamy photos from her past lover. Of course, he has a price for returning those pictures, but it's not money he's after. *The Sultan's Bed,* by Laura Wright, continues the tales of her sheikh heroes with an enigmatic male who is searching for his missing sister and finds a startling attraction to her lovely neighbor. And finally, what was supposed to be just an elevator ride turns into a very passionate encounter, in *Blame It on the Blackout* by Heidi Betts.

Sit back and enjoy all of the smart, sensual stories Silhouette Desire has to offer.

Happy reading,

Melissa Jeglinski

Melissa Jeglinski
Senior Editor
Silhouette Desire

Please address questions and book requests to:
Silhouette Reader Service
U.S.: 3010 Walden Ave., P.O. Box 1325, Buffalo, NY 14269
Canadian: P.O. Box 609, Fort Erie, Ont. L2A 5X3

ESTATE AFFAIR
Sara Orwig

Published by Silhouette Books

America's Publisher of Contemporary Romance

With thanks to Melissa Jeglinski

Special thanks and acknowledgment are given to
Sara Orwig for her contribution
to the DYNASTIES: THE ASHTONS series.

 SILHOUETTE BOOKS

ISBN 0-373-76657-2

ESTATE AFFAIR

Copyright © 2005 by Harlequin Books S.A.

Visit Silhouette Books at www.eHarlequin.com

Printed in U.S.A.

Books by Sara Orwig

Silhouette Desire

Falcon's Lair #938
The Bride's Choice #1019
A Baby for Mommy #1060
Babes in Arms #1094
Her Torrid Temporary Marriage #1125
The Consummate Cowboy #1164
The Cowboy's Seductive Proposal #1192
World's Most Eligible Texan #1346
Cowboy's Secret Child #1368
The Playboy Meets His Match #1438
Cowboy's Special Woman #1449
*Do You Take This Enemy? #1476
*The Rancher, the Baby & the Nanny #1486
Entangled with a Texan #1547
†Shut Up and Kiss Me #1581
†Standing Outside the Fire #1594
Estate Affair #1657

Silhouette Intimate Moments

Hide in Plain Sight #679
Galahad in Blue Jeans #971
*One Tough Cowboy #1192
†Bring on the Night #1298
†Don't Close Your Eyes #1316

*Stallion Pass
†Stallion Pass: Texas Knights

SARA ORWIG

lives in Oklahoma. She has a patient husband who will take her on research trips anywhere from big cities to old forts. She is an avid collector of Western history books. With a master's degree in English, Sara has written historical romance, mainstream fiction and contemporary romance. Books are beloved treasures that take Sara to magical worlds, and she loves both reading and writing them.

THE ASHTONS

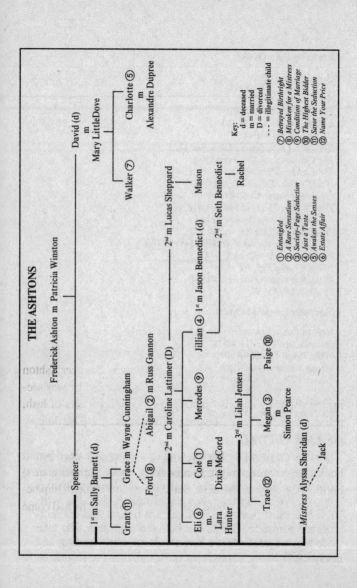

Frederick Ashton m Patricia Winston

Spencer — David (d) m Mary LittleDove

1st m Sally Barnett (d)

Grant ⑪ — Grace m Wayne Cunningham — Abigail ② m Russ Gannon

Ford ⑧

Walker ⑦ — Charlotte ⑤ m Alexandre Dupree

2nd m Caroline Lattimer (D)

2nd m Lucas Sheppard

Eli ⑥ m. Lara Hunter — Cole ① m Dixie McCord — Mercedes ⑨ — Jillian ④ 1st m Jason Bennedict (d) — Mason — Rachel

2nd m Seth Bennedict

3rd m Lilah Jensen

Trace ⑫ — Megan ③ m Simon Pearce — Paige ⑩

Mistress Alyssa Sheridan (d) - - - Jack

Key:
d = deceased
m = married
D = divorced
- - - = illegitimate child

① Entangled
② A Rare Sensation
③ Society-Page Seduction
④ Just a Taste
⑤ Awaken the Senses
⑥ Estate Affair
⑦ Betrayed Birthright
⑧ Mistaken for a Mistress
⑨ Condition of Marriage
⑩ The Highest Bidder
⑪ Savor the Seduction
⑫ Name Your Price

Prologue

June 1976

It was an unpleasant task but he needed to do it tonight. Standing in the library of his home in San Francisco, Spencer Ashton gazed out the night-darkened window. In his mind he was seeing the Ashton vineyard—in daylight—acre upon acre of lush, prime-producing vines bearing Pinot Noir and Chardonnay grapes.

His gaze roamed the library, with its shelves of leather-bound books; oil paintings in gilt frames on the walls; leather chairs; his immaculate, massive desk. Satisfaction shot through him because now his wealth would soar. What a long way he had come from Crawley, Nebraska!

At the sound of the door opening, his wife appeared. She rarely came to the library, and the children were forbidden to enter it. Spencer had proclaimed this room his domain, a haven from his family.

His gaze raked over Caroline. She wore a pink dress, typical for her. Ordinary and insipid. After tonight he would be rid of her for good. Distaste filled him. His only regret was that his split with her couldn't happen faster.

"You wanted to talk," Caroline said, her hazel-green eyes gazing at him.

"Yes, come in," he replied, thinking how mousy she was. Not the woman for him. Maybe at one time he'd been attracted to her and thought she might be exciting enough to hold his interest, but that feeling had soon been dispelled. Yet she'd been the means for acquiring what he'd wanted. and she'd served his purposes well.

Entering the room, she gazed up at him. "What is it, Spencer?"

"I'm leaving you, Caroline," he stated bluntly, glad to finally break their ties. "Our marriage is finished—but then it's been finished for quite some time."

She paled and flinched as if he had hit her, and his distaste deepened. Why was she acting surprised, he wondered. How could she have hoped to hold him?

"Leaving me!" she repeated as if she couldn't hear well. "Spencer, we have four small children—we took vows."

"I've filed for divorce. It's already done and will be in the paper tomorrow. I thought you would prefer to hear it from me first."

"You didn't discuss this—"

"There's nothing to discuss. I want out of this marriage. I'm taking the Lattimer Corporation stock with me, Caroline. Your father willed his shares of the investment banking business to me," Spencer declared, getting to the heart of the matter.

"You can't do that!" she cried, trembling badly. "My father left everything to you in good faith. As my husband and father of our children, his grandchildren, he bequeathed land and stock and money to you. He didn't give it to you to take everything away from his daughter and grandchildren! I won't let you do that!"

Her eyes flashed with a fire that surprised Spencer. He had expected her to burst into tears and plead and beg. Instead her fists were clenched, and she was shaking. Except for bright spots of color in her cheeks, she was deathly pale.

"Caroline, he bequeathed it all to me. Everything is mine. End of argument."

"I'll get my lawyer, and we'll see about ending this discussion. I'll contest the will. You can't take your children's heritage and my life support from us!"

"Think not?" He didn't like opposition and hadn't expected any argument from her. Spencer stepped closer to her, angrily grasping her shoulders and digging his fingers in until she flinched. "If you try to stop me, I'll take the children from you and you'll have nothing. I have people on our staff who will, if I want, testify that you're on drugs."

"That's a lie! I've never done anything like that!"

"These people will testify under oath that you have."

"You'll pay them to lie!" she cried, her voice rising. "It'll all be lies!"

"You can't keep me from getting everything your father passed down to me. Believe me, Caroline, I'm prepared. I can get the children and the estate and you'll have absolutely nothing."

"You're pure evil, Spencer!" she exclaimed in a low voice. "You can't take my children!" The tears did come now, spilling down her cheeks just as he had expected, while she trembled violently.

He dropped his hands.

"You do one thing to contest the will and you'll never see the children. Do you understand that, Caroline?" he snapped, furious that she was threatening him. He would ruin her if she interfered with him!

Caroline stared hard at Spencer through her tears. She'd been so wrong about this man, her husband. She'd known something between them was never right, that he was cold to their children, but she'd hung on for their sake. But now she saw him for what he truly was. A cold, heartless and calculating bastard. He'd never cared about her. Never cared about his own children. All he'd ever wanted was her inheritance. And she'd been fool enough to fall for his lies. He didn't deserve her tears.

"I can see you for what you truly are now, Spencer," she said, her voice shaking from fear and anger. "I can see that you don't deserve the children. They deserve so much more. I can't stop you from taking what my father left you, but I *can* raise *my* children to be honest and loving and have integrity. I can teach them to be nothing like you. And I still have the vineyard my mother left me. You can't touch that. So go, if you must. Perhaps you are doing us all a favor."

Stunned, Spencer stared at Caroline and saw something in her eyes he'd never seen before: strength.

Shrugging off the odd feeling this produced, he said, "You agree to accept my terms without a fight?"

Caroline squared her shoulders, even as fresh tears fell from her eyes. "Yes."

Spencer's pulse pounded with enthusiasm and victory. He was free of her and the children! He didn't ever want to see any of them again. He swept into the hall and almost collided with his oldest son.

Eight-year-old Eli Ashton gazed up at Spencer with round eyes, his skin as pale as his mother's. For a startled instant Spencer and his son stared at each other, and then Eli flew at him.

"I hate you!" he cried, his small fists doubled as he leaped at Spencer and pounded him.

Spencer swung his hand, his palm cracking against Eli's cheek, sending the child sprawling. Spencer headed to the door, where he'd left the bags he'd already packed. And then he left, turning his back on Caroline and the children forever.

One

Twenty-Nine Years Later

Who killed Spencer Ashton? Eli Ashton's gaze drifted over the remaining mourners who had come to the Ashton Estate to give condolences to the family at the funeral reception. The event was winding down, yet the family was still busy talking to friends and hadn't noticed Eli's presence. When and if they did, he was certain he would be asked to leave.

How many of these people had really liked Spencer? Eli thought his father's enemies were probably legion.

He was the only one of his family who had come to the funeral reception at the Ashton Estate and he knew why. Not one of them was welcome. The tension between the two families at the funeral had been palpable. But curiosity had overcome him and he had to see the house that should have been, and once was, his mother's. His grandfather's house and vineyards. All stolen by Spencer, Eli thought bitterly.

Jamming his clenched fist into the pants pocket of his charcoal suit, he strolled across the large reception hall and stepped outside onto the veranda. Beyond the manicured gardens were acres of lush green vineyards. As head winemaker for his family's vineyards, Eli knew the vines would be going into fruit set and already have tiny green grapes. It was the first of June in a season that, so far, had been good.

His gaze ran over the vineyards again and the knot of anger inside him tightened. All of this stolen from his mother! All of his family rejected by Spencer. And now, Grant Ashton, Spencer's first-born son, had turned up from Nebraska. The scandalous news had broken of Spencer's first marriage. A marriage that had never been dissolved. Spencer had committed bigamy, Eli thought. Legally Spencer shouldn't have been able to inherit this estate, mansion, vineyards, any of it.

"Sir, do you need anything?" a woman asked.

Eli barely glanced at her out of the corner of his eye. "I need a lot of things. Right now, solitude. I came out here hoping I would be left alone," he replied, clamping his jaw closed and knowing he needed to control his anger. He raked his fingers through his straight, brown hair. He had been too abrupt, but he didn't want to talk to a stranger.

"And I thought all the big egos were inside," came the soft reply.

Startled, Eli forgot his anger. He turned to look at the woman who was heading back into the house. Taking a quick inventory, he observed long shapely legs, high-heeled pumps, a sleeveless black dress that ended above her knees. Thick auburn curls were looped and pinned on her head. The tendrils that had managed to escape made him think about running his fingers through her hair.

"So, when you stir up the heat, you run?" he drawled.

She stopped and turned around slowly, as if she had all the time in the world to deal with him. The moment their gazes met, he could feel electricity snap between them. She strolled toward him, and her sensual, languorous movement made his pulse jump. When he looked into her light honey-brown eyes, with the thickest lashes he had ever seen, his breath quickened. Her eyes captivated him. As she slowly approached him, he saw sparks dancing in their depths. She had a sexy walk, a slight sway of her hips, but it was the provocation in her eyes that kept his pulse racing.

"Nothing you can do will make me run," she replied with conviction.

"Nothing?" he drawled, moving closer to her. "That's an interesting statement and conjures up all sorts of things I'd like to do."

"Like what?" she challenged, her eyes carrying their own defiance She was self-confident, intriguing.

"Like hold you in my arms and feel your softness against me. Like taste your lips in a slow, wet kiss," he confessed in a husky voice, a little surprised at his own admission. He didn't normally behave this way with women he didn't know. But she'd opened the door and invited him in. "For starters, I'd like to have a drink with you, and later, dinner," he replied.

"We're total strangers. I don't do that," she answered coolly, stopping only a few feet from him.

"We can remedy that quickly. I'm Eli," he said, extending his hand. "And you are—" he asked.

When she held out her hand, he grasped warm, slender fingers. The heat between them burned even hotter when they touched. It sent a current straight to his nether regions, while his gaze slipped down to her full, rosy lips.

"I'm Lara," she replied.

What would it be like to feel those lips against his, he wondered. "I didn't think I'd be around any firecrackers until next month, but now I see I was wrong," he said.

"Me? A firecracker!" She laughed with a dazzling smile and a flash of even, white teeth. "All I did was rock your quiet, climate-controlled world a tiny bit." He still held her hand while their gazes remained locked, feeling the same sizzling results.

"Let's get out of here and have a drink together," he said, and took her arm, touching her so lightly, feeling the contact to his toes. She smelled enticing, and then he recognized the perfume. For a second she hesitated. "Let's go, Lara," he repeated, liking the sound of her name. "You know you want to," he added.

"You're dangerous," she said softly.

"No, I'm not," he replied, touching her slender throat. "Your pulse is racing and you want to go."

She ran her index finger across his wrist, a slow, sensual stroke while pinpoints of fire danced in the depths of her gaze. "I think your pulse is racing, too."

"If we can do that to each other already, then we *have* to get to know each other," he said, linking her arm through his, knowing he wasn't ready to let her out of his sight.

"You're incredibly sure of yourself."

"Right now, I'm sure about both of us," he replied. He rarely acted impulsively, but he wanted to spend time with her, and they needed to get away from the Ashton Estate. He wanted her to himself. His gaze drifted down over her, over her slender throat and lush curves. He wanted to peel away that black dress and see what was beneath. "Let's go," he said, holding her arm as he took a step.

"All right, Eli, I'll throw caution to the wind and act on impulse. Don't make me regret it." She fell into step beside him. He was intently aware of her at his side, her head coming to just slightly above his shoulder.

"Midnight Desire," he said softly, and as she glanced up, her eyes widened.

"You know my perfume!" Lara exclaimed in surprise. "You must know a lot of women to identify a perfume quickly like that."

"No. It's not women in my life. I have a nose for scents. And I have sisters."

"Sisters—right," she said, obviously dubious of his declaration.

He directed her to a shiny, black sports car. When he opened the passenger door for her, Lara slid into the seat and watched him as he walked around the car. He was ruggedly handsome with riveting green eyes, but it wasn't just his appealing looks or his green eyes that had her seated in his car.

It was this breathtaking, hot attraction and her curiosity about him. He was mysterious and intriguing. He had been harsh on the veranda when he'd snapped at her, but she hadn't been any better with her smart-mouthed reply. She blamed the strain of the emotional day for her loss of control. She'd expected him to ignore her, but instead he had given her a challenge that she couldn't ignore. Now here she was in his elegant sports car, going to dinner with him.

She ran her hand over the soft, brown leather that covered the seat. She had never been in such a splendid car or with a man as exciting as Eli, yet she knew that she was out of her element with him. So far out of her element that she should get out of the car and go back where she belonged. She was an Ashton maid, domestic help, and when the fall semester started, a college student. Whatever he did, she guessed he was wealthy. But he was too enticing to pass up, and just this once she wanted to be with a dashing, stimulating man, riding in his fancy car, tossing aside cares and enjoying the moment.

When he slid onto the seat beside her and started the engine, she caught a whiff of his aftershave. She shifted, adjusting her seat belt so she could watch him. His profile was to her and she drank in the sight of him, looking at his brown hair, fantasizing about running her fingers through the thick strands.

They circled a glistening pond in the center of the drive and sped away from the mansion. When he had to stop to turn onto the highway, he glanced at her.

"You drive as if you have a destination in mind," she said.

"I always have a destination in mind," he replied. "There's a bar overlooking the Napa River where we can have a drink and talk. Later, we can have dinner together." He touched her hand. "You don't have a wedding ring, so you're single. Is there a particular man in your life right now?"

"No, there's not. And you don't have a ring, either."

"And there's no particular woman in my life. At least not until the past half hour."

She laughed. "I wouldn't say I'm 'in your life.'"

"Yes, you are," he insisted in his deep masculine voice. "And I intend to keep you there," he declared. She inhaled, knowing his words were ridiculous and yet unable to resist them. He was temptation, excitement, a sexy male.

"Do you always go after what you want with this much determination?"

One of his dark eyebrows arched. "You have no idea."

"So, Eli, let me guess what you do. You're too well-fixed to have a laborer's job. You have that look of money. At the same time you look as if you're accustomed to doing rough, physical activities."

"What's the look of money?"

"Your elegant sports car. Your fine suit."

"What makes you think I do physical work?"

She wondered if she was far off the mark, yet that was the way he appeared to her. He kept a barrier up and didn't reveal much of himself. She couldn't tell whether her analysis amused or annoyed him.

"I'll have to admit that when you linked my arm in yours, I felt your muscles. You didn't get them sitting behind a desk."

"I could sit behind a desk and work out at a gym and get muscles," he replied.

"No. You're deeply tanned. I'm betting that you do something physical," she said. He had revealed a rough edge on the veranda at the Ashton Estate that ruled out a myriad of professions. "Whatever you do, you're successful at it," she said.

"Where did you get that idea? My car and my suit?"

"Not at all. Your self-assurance."

He gave her a sardonic glance. "Enough about me. I'm a winemaker," he said. "Now, speaking of walking—" he reached over and drew his fingers along her arm, sending tingles spiraling in the wake of his touch "—you have a walk that is sexy enough to set a man ablaze."

"I don't set men on fire," she replied, feeling her cheeks flush.

"We can argue that one when I'm not driving."

Could she possibly send this man into flames? She couldn't imagine it. Her gaze roamed down his long legs and then back up to find him watching her, before he returned his attention to the road.

When they sped into Napa, anticipation fizzed in her veins. As they drove down Main Street, passing Victorian-style houses, she looked at the town she had known most of her life, yet now she saw it as if for the first time. They passed the Jarvis Conservatory that had been so pretty when the wisteria vines had been in bloom earlier. She looked at the plain Vintners' Collective Building, and in minutes they drove past the renovated opera house with its cheerful red awning. Crossing the winding Napa River, she saw a red and green Napa trolley as it rumbled along the street.

Because of the man beside her, the sky seemed bluer, the air fresher. Colors were more vivid, impressions carving into her memory in a day she would never forget. Gone was the emotional, depressing day with the funeral and all it involved. Now she felt full of life, anticipation bubbling in her.

In minutes they were seated on a terrace that overlooked a bend in the glistening Napa River. Tables were covered in white linen cloths, centered with vases of fresh daisies and roses. Orange and yellow nasturtiums filled pots along the terrace, while multicolored flowers spilled from hanging baskets and a musician played softly from somewhere inside the restaurant.

Eli ordered a bottle of Chardonnay and appetizers. Their white-coated waiter uncorked the wine and waited for Eli's approval. After pouring their glasses, the waiter left to return with the appetizers Eli had ordered.

Eli raised his glass. "Here's to us, Lara," he said quietly.

He leaned across the table and drew his fingers over her knuckles. "I want to take you to dinner Saturday night," he said. "We can go dancing."

"I need to know you better," she replied, a smile curving her full lips.

He touched the corner of her mouth.

"I like your smile, Lara. And we will know each other a lot better by Saturday. We can start right now. Tell me what you like to do and what you don't like."

"I like the usual things that everyone likes—dancing, swimming, reading. There's nothing unusual about me."

"That's not so," he said firmly. "Your brown eyes are unusually beautiful."

"Oh, please!" she exclaimed. Lara smiled at him, yet his compliment pleased her. He leaned closer while the fingers of his right hand lightly stroked back and forth across her knuckles. If anyone had unusually beautiful eyes, he did. Thickly lashed, filled with emerald fire, they were bedroom eyes, spellbinding eyes.

"Don't deny it. I've never seen eyes that shade of milk chocolate with golden flecks in their depths. Everything about you has been unusual, which is why I'm intrigued and intend to know you better."

She smiled at him, shaking her head. "I think you are having a reaction to the gloomy day we've had."

He traced his fingers along the corner of her mouth while he shook his head in denial. "Not at all. I will get to know you. I promise you that."

As his declarations sent her pulse racing, she wondered if anything in his adult life had ever stopped him or been unattainable for him.

"Try this dip," he said, spooning some on a cracker and holding it out. "Take a bite." She reached up to take the cracker from him, but he caught her hand with his free one. "Take a bite," he repeated in a low voice, still holding the tidbit.

She leaned forward to let him feed it to her. This brought her only inches from him, heightening her desire. His finger barely brushed her lip, and all the time, his gaze held hers. He was sexy, commanding.

"Maybe I'd better feed myself," she said in a breathless voice, looking at his sensual, well-sculpted mouth.

As the shadows lengthened, the sun became a fireball on the western horizon, splintering golden reflections across the swiftly running river. Tables around them filled and the noise level rose, although she barely noticed anyone else. Lara's world held only Eli and her.

"Lara," he said, turning her hand in his and leaning closer across the table. "Let's have dinner alone. Let me get a suite and we'll have dinner sent up and we can be together without all this," Eli said, waving his hand at those around them.

While the question, and all it implied, hung in the air, she looked into his green eyes and found them full of unspoken promises of passion.

Two

Lara inhaled deeply. She had to make a choice. Common sense told her to refuse, yet when she gazed into his seductive bedroom eyes, she knew she wanted the same thing he did. Why did it seem so right to be with him? She didn't want the evening to end, and the thought of getting a suite had her heart pounding.

He raised her hand and brushed a feathery kiss across her palm and then looked at her for an answer.

"Yes, Eli," she said softly. "A suite would be exciting."

He paid the bill, left a generous tip and then held her chair. She preceded him across the terrace until they reached the sidewalk. Eli took her hand and they walked a few doors down to a red brick five-story hotel that overlooked the river.

In the lobby he turned to her. "Wait here while I register us," he said.

She nodded, her pulse racing as she watched him walk away.

His features were rugged, yet softened by his thick eyelashes and emerald eyes. He had a purposeful walk, but then, he'd told her over drinks that he always had a destination. He was a man who knew where he was going and wasted no time getting there. And yet, for the past few hours he had given her his whole, undivided attention, hanging on every word she said as if she were rare and special. And she had done the same with him.

She shifted her weight and wondered about the attraction that had exploded between them the first time they looked at each other. Impossible. Only, it had happened and was still occurring. Right now her pulse was racing, and she didn't want to stop looking at him and she longed to run her fingers through his thick, brown hair. She wanted to kiss him.

Her heart thudded on that one. She wondered if she knew herself.

Then he was walking back to her and all thoughts fled as he took her arm.

Along with the bellman they rode the elevator to the top floor. The bellman opened the suite door and switched on lights for them.

While Eli tipped the man, she strolled into the sitting room of their spacious suite. A large bouquet of fresh flowers was centered on a fruitwood table in front of a grouping of chairs covered in off-white damask. One end of the room to her right held a small kitchen and between the kitchen and the sitting room was a dining area. To her left, she glimpsed a bedroom.

On thick, white carpet she crossed the room to the floor-to-ceiling windows to look at the view of the river and the mountains beyond it. The sun was sliding lower, and dark would soon descend.

Eli turned to her and she saw the white-hot desire in his eyes. "Now, isn't this better?" he asked, shedding his coat and dropping it on a chair. Before she could answer, there was a knock at the door and a male voice announced, "Room service."

The bellman set a tray on the table. It held an iced bottle of champagne, glasses and a fruit tray with bright red strawberries, yellow chunks of pineapple, slices of green kiwi and purple grapes. As pretty as the fruit looked, her appetite had vanished earlier in the day and had not yet returned.

When he was gone, Eli poured them both glasses of champagne.

Lara thought she might as well be in a dream, only this was real, but like nothing she had ever done before. She had fallen into a fairy-tale afternoon, taken out of her ordinary life like Cinderella by her prince. And for the next few hours, Lara decided she was going to continue to enjoy every minute *and* the sexy man who'd conjured it.

"I've never done anything so impulsive in my life," she said.

"Neither have I, Lara," he replied solemnly. "But this is different."

She wondered how it was different for him and if he were telling her the truth. She couldn't imagine a man like Eli hadn't had all kinds of experiences with women. Women far more sophisticated, beautiful and with the same lifestyle as his.

He raised the flute of champagne. "Here's to a fantastic evening," he said.

She touched her glass to his, hearing the faint clink and then she sipped the bubbling, golden liquid.

"Now, isn't this a lot better," he said, unfastening his conservative charcoal tie and tossing it on a nearby chair.

"Yes, it's better, but probably not the wisest thing I've done," she replied. As he unbuttoned the top two buttons of his white shirt, her throat went dry.

"I think it's one of the best things I've ever done," he said, his enigmatic eyes darkening. He reached out to pull a pin from her hair and let a lock tumble to her shoulder. With deliberation he removed another pin. His fingers tugging gently on pins fueled the fires building in her. "This is what I wanted to see," he whispered while his gaze roamed over her. "Your hair is magnificent."

She had never been told that before. In minutes her hair was free of pins, framing her face in a silky cascade that poured over her shoulders.

He took her glass from her hand and set it on the table next to his. Then, as he reached for her, she walked eagerly into his arms, wrapping her arms around his neck. Her heart drummed. Caution had gone out the window when she left the estate with him, and now she wanted to kiss him, wanted to explore and discover and be kissed.

Lean and hard, he was solid muscle. He smelled of a tantalizing aftershave that she could not recognize. His strong arms banded her waist as he looked down at her. "I've been wanting to hold you since I first looked into your eyes."

Before today, she would have thought a line like that would be pure fabrication, but with this man, she believed him. There was no mistaking the blatant need in his eyes. He gazed at her with a hunger that made her breathless.

She reached up with her forefinger and traced his lower lip. He inhaled deeply, and she was amazed at the effect she had on him. He reacted to her slightest touch.

"Lara," he said, his voice gravelly, "I want you."

She pulled him closer, and his eyelids became hooded. As his gaze lowered to her mouth, he leaned the last few inches to touch the corner of her mouth lightly with the tip of his tongue.

The contact sizzled. Her lips felt swollen, aching to discover his. She wound her fingers in his thick hair.

"I've wanted to do this all day," he whispered. He lowered his head and his mouth brushed hers. Seconds later, his tongue parted her lips, sliding into her mouth.

She returned his kiss, her tongue stroking his slowly. He was equally deliberate, launching a searing exploration of her mouth.

She'd never been kissed like this. She shook with fiery longing. Her fingers dug into his back and held on tightly.

One of his arms circled her waist while he shifted enough to be able to let one of his hands cruise across her breasts. Through the cotton dress and the wispy bra beneath, his caress was a lightning bolt streaking over her raw nerves. Her nipples were already tight, but his touch made them tingle, even through two layers of clothes—and made her ache to be free of the constriction.

Her fingers went to the buttons on his shirt to twist them loose until she could run her hand across his chest. She tangled her fingers in the thick brown hair on his chest, then brushed her hands across his flat nipples.

At her touch, he gasped and dipped his head to claim her mouth in another scalding kiss.

His free hand roamed over her bottom.

She tugged his shirt out of his pants, unbuttoned it and then pushed it off his broad shoulders. She paused, opening her eyes with an effort to meet his hooded gaze.

She leaned back to let her eyes feast on him. He was thick through the shoulders and chest, his body tapering down to narrow hips. The mat of brown curls narrowed down to a fine line that disappeared below his belt.

His belt. She wanted to unfasten it and free him of the constraint of his trousers. She glanced up to meet his scorching gaze again. He took her shoulders and turned her, leaning forward to let his warm breath play over her nape. Then his tongue followed as he brushed kisses on her nape. His fingers tugged her zipper down, his tongue following the opening to her waist.

Turning her to face him again, Eli pushed her black dress off her shoulders.

It floated to the floor in a puddle around her ankles, but her attention was on him as his gaze lowered to her breasts.

"Oh, yes," he whispered. "You're perfection." He reached out to brush her nipples.

She gasped with pleasure and wrapped her arms around him, kissing him. He placed a light hand on her midriff, stopping her.

"I want to look at you, Lara." He ground out the words when she looked at him questioningly. "I want to savor you, to explore you, to kiss you. I want to know you as I know myself, to know your softness, your body, your reactions. I intend to learn what pleases you and what excites you," he drawled, his stated intentions heightening her fervor. "This night I want to drive you wild."

His words aroused her almost as much as his caresses inflamed her. This handsome, dashing man was sinfully tempting. She could barely think or talk, but she wanted the same thing he did. She wanted to discover all of him, to know him tonight as she had never known a man before. Then his kisses tracing her throat took her attention.

All she wore now was her pink bra and cotton panties that were cut low across her stomach. She wore thigh-high hose, and he reached out to roll them down. His fingers caressed her leg as he slid first one stocking and then the other off.

He stood and brushed her nipples with his fingers. The taut buds pushed against the fabric, and she shook with need.

Reaching out to touch his belt, she slid her hands to the

buckle to unfasten it and then unzipped his trousers to free him from constraints. She reached out to tug down his briefs, inhaling deeply at the sight of his manhood. Thick and hard, he was ready for her. "Eli," she whispered, stroking him.

With a groan he turned to her again, leaning down to trail warm kisses on her throat, nibbling on her earlobe while he unsnapped the clasp to her bra and pushed it away. As he cupped each full globe, she moaned.

Then his head went lower, seeking her pink, pouty nipples and letting his tongue circle first one and then the other. He pulled her partially against him, his tanned arm dark against her pale skin where he circled her waist. While he continued to kiss her breast, his hand drifted down over her stomach to push down her panties and reveal the thick auburn curls at the juncture of her thighs.

She trembled, nipping at his neck, kissing his shoulder, running her hands across his chest again.

He knelt in front of her, his fingers feathering along the inside of her thighs while he spread kisses across her stomach.

His tongue made burning paths on the inside of first one thigh and then the other. Closing her eyes, she clutched his shoulders tightly. Sensations rocked her. His fingers moved to her most intimate places, sliding through her thick auburn curls, to caress her.

She cried out when he increased the pressure of his fingers, finding the bud that was supremely sensitive. She moved her hips, lost now in mounting desire. While he kissed and rubbed her, his other hand glided down. His forefinger slid inside her, and her cry was muffled by his mouth. She hadn't known she could want a man to the extent she wanted him—or respond to one with the abandon he was driving her to.

When he stopped, she cried out, wanting more, consumed by

the need he had created. Hunger for him tore at her. She clutched his waist as he stood and looked at her, smoothing her hair away from her face with one hand and caressing her breast with the other. "What do you want, Lara?" he whispered. "Tell me."

"You are driving me wild and you know it. Oh, please," she said, all inhibitions gone, melted away by his hot loving. "Put your hand back on me," she whispered, caressing his throbbing rod.

He pulled her close to kiss her, a devastating kiss where his tongue thrust deeply and slowly, then withdrew, repeating the thrusts with deliberation, imitating the sex act. Clutching his shoulders, she dug her fingers into his back.

His leg pushed between hers, a roughness against her smooth folds, and she gasped. "Ride me, Lara," he whispered in her ear, his warm breath tickling her as his tongue followed the curve of her ear.

She clung to him, knowing she was wanton and not caring. He had driven her mad with his mouth and fingers, and now the exquisite pressure of his leg between hers was taking her to a brink. Her hips thrust wildly while he kissed her again hard. She closed her hand around his manhood, stroking him, but barely aware of what she was doing. All her being focused now on needs created by his leg between hers.

"You like that, Lara?" he whispered, and then kissed her again.

She couldn't answer, but gasped for breath as the need for a climax tore at her. She clutched at him and cried out.

"That's it! Ahh, Lara," he exclaimed. "I want to drive you wild."

She barely heard him. Her pulse roared and she was caught by a power that she couldn't control. While her hips gyrated on him, he increased the pressure of his leg between her thighs.

Release exploded in her, lights playing behind her closed eyelids.

"Sweet," he whispered against her mouth and put his fingers where his leg had been, building another storm. Urgency drove her as frantically as before until she burst over the brink.

"I want you, Eli!" she gasped, standing on tiptoe and pulling his head up to kiss him. His strong arms banded her tightly, holding her softness against her hard strength. She felt his hot erection pressing against her stomach. Framing his face with her hands, she tore her lips from his. "I want you inside me," she whispered, and his chest expanded as he inhaled deeply. His head dipped to kiss her again while his hands cupped her full breasts.

His thumbs circled her nipples slowly, tantalizing touches that fanned desire until it was white-hot. She knelt, looking up at him briefly, drinking in the sight of this ruggedly handsome man who went after what he wanted with all of his concentration. His thighs were hard, his stomach ridged with muscles.

She caressed his manhood, touching him with her tongue, circling the velvet tip and then finally taking him in her mouth.

He groaned and his fingers wound tightly in her hair while she sucked and kissed him and stroked him with her tongue. Her hand went between his legs to caress him, cupping him and touching sensitive skin.

Within seconds he yanked her up to kiss her passionately and then picked her up into his arms.

"It's never been like this," she whispered, astounded at the fireworks he set off in her.

Closing her eyes again, she wound her arms around his neck. He walked to the bedroom and placed her on the bed to roll her over on her stomach.

He moved to her feet, spreading her legs apart. She twisted around, wanting her hands and mouth on him. "Eli—"

"Shh, Lara. Let me kiss you," he said, running his hands along the inside of her legs. His tongue followed. She clutched the bed and closed her eyes, bombarded again by sensations that fanned raging fires.

He moved higher between her legs and his fingers slipped over her bottom, lingering while his tongue stroked the inside of her thigh until she spread her legs wide. Aching for him, she tried to turn over, but his hand in the small of her back held her gently.

"Wait, Lara. Let me learn what you like. Do you like this?" he said, his tongue dawdled along the inside of her thigh. "Do you?" he persisted while he continued to caress and kiss her.

"Yes!" she cried. He was nipping now, the faint stubble of his beard tickling her bottom. Then he shifted, letting her roll over. He moved between her legs and placed her hands high over her head. Then he drew his fingers down over her palms, her arms, down over her underarms to her breasts.

By this time she was straining toward him, and he circled one nipple with his fingers while he leaned down to take her other nipple into his mouth, biting slightly, just enough to make her gasp with pleasure.

Lara had never known desire as she did now. She wanted him with an overwhelming, consuming need that drove all else from her mind. All she could think about was Eli.

"I want you, Eli!" she cried. "I want you inside me!"

"I'll get protection," he promised, stepping off the bed and taking his billfold from his trousers to get out a packet. She put her hands behind her head to watch him, his male body creating sensual anticipation. As he approached the bed, she reached out to caress his hip.

He leaned forward to kiss her and then moved between her legs. He was virile and rugged, tanned to his waist from days in the sun. He lowered himself, and she wrapped her long legs around him, pulling him to her to kiss him while she ran her hand down his smooth back and over his hard buttocks.

He entered her slowly, withdrawing and then sliding into her again. She arched and tightened her legs. "Eli," she urged, "I want you."

"Lara," he murmured and filled her, hot and hard. He kissed her again as she thrust her hips and they moved together.

She knew he was exerting control, holding back to love her longer, but she thought she would come apart if she didn't reach a climax soon. She slid her hands down to his buttocks and pulled him more tightly to her. In minutes she could tell that his control was slipping away. Then it was gone, and he pumped hard and fast.

She burst with release. Clinging to him, she continued to move her hips while he still was thrusting, and in seconds urgency built in her again.

Moving with him, ecstasy once again exploded in her. Her cries were muffled by his kisses as he shuddered with satisfaction. While his thrusts slowed, they both gasped for breath. She could feel that his pounding heart was racing as fast as hers.

Kissing him, Lara held him tightly. Her legs were locked around him as she slid her hands up and down his back slowly, moving them lower over his bare buttocks, wanting to put her hands everywhere on his marvelous body.

This spellbinding, rugged man had whisked her away for one enchanted night that she would always remember. She knew she had to go back to her ordinary life, but right now, a Prince Charming—with some rough edges, but nonetheless, Prince

Charming—had loved her right out of her mind. And she suspected she had taken him along with her.

He turned to shower light kisses on her temple, stroking her hair from her face, and then he rolled onto his side, keeping her close so he could look at her.

"What you do to me is awesome," he said, studying her with such a solemn expression she wondered what was really running through his mind.

"It's mutual," she whispered, feathering her fingers along his jaw, delighting in touching him and loving the intimacy they were sharing.

"You melted my bones. I'm jelly now."

She poked his chest with her forefinger. "You don't feel like jelly," she said, and he grinned.

"Believe me, I am. If the hotel catches on fire, you may have to carry me out."

She laughed. "If the hotel catches on fire now, we're both in trouble. I'm not sure I can find all my clothes."

"They're here. I remember taking them off you," he said, his voice dropping a notch. He met her gaze and she wondered what he was thinking as she gazed into his unfathomable green eyes. He combed her hair away from her face and propped his head on his hand, leaning on his elbow to look down at her. Locks of his brown hair fell over his forehead, and the stubble of his beard faintly showed.

"You're beautiful, Lara," he said.

Her heart thudded with his compliment, and she ran her fingers along his strong shoulder. "Thank you. I'm glad you think so, but at this moment, it's the sex talking."

"No. At this moment I'm seeing more clearly than ever. Desire is temporarily banked and I can take an objective look. I'm also becoming aware that I have a stomach. We didn't drink the wine or eat the appetizers or drink our champagne. I'm ready for room service and I'd like to sink my teeth into—" he paused and looked down to draw his fingers over the rise of her breast.

"Into what?" she asked breathlessly.

He leaned down to nuzzle her neck, awakening new tingles in her. He shifted, tracing kisses lower on her stomach. Then he raised his head and slid off the bed. He bent over to pick her up in his arms.

When he did, Lara wrapped her arms around his neck. "We're going somewhere?" she asked, amused and curious.

"I think it's time for a shower, and then we can study the menu and decide what we want and order it up."

"Suppose what I want is a tall, dark, handsome man?" she asked.

He arched one dark eyebrow. "I don't know where I'll find him, and I can tell you now, I'm not interested in looking for another guy for you."

"You're handsome. All right then, a tall, dark, sexy man. How's that?"

He grinned. "Hopefully I can conjure up that man."

"We'll see what you can conjure *up,*" she said in a suggestive drawl, and he smiled.

They entered a large black marble bathroom with a huge tub and gold fixtures. He carried Lara to the shower and stepped inside, setting her on her feet.

"We're doing this together?" she asked.

"Absolutely," he replied. "I'm ready. Are you?"

She felt his arousal against her stomach. Her gaze roamed down the length of him. "I'll say you're ready!"

His gaze glowed with pinpoints of steaming desire. "Why don't we do something about it?"

"I'd say I'm ready, too," she whispered, her voice fading. She scooted closer, slipped her arm around his neck and stood on tiptoe to kiss him. His arm banded her waist and he held her tightly.

Urgency tore at them as if desire hadn't been surfeited only a short time ago. Eli wanted her with a need that shocked him. He should be satisfied. Just minutes ago he didn't think he could move a muscle. Now desire enveloped him, stronger than ever. He framed her face with his hands. She was beautiful, with rosy skin, a smattering of freckles across her nose and that riotous mass of auburn hair shot through with brighter red strands.

He cupped her full breasts with both hands and stroked her nipples with his thumbs. Her intense responses to his lovemaking set him on fire, and he had never been so turned on by a woman's kisses.

When the water was on, he handed her soap, and they soaped each other slowly. His hands meandered over her while her every gasp heightened his need.

They rinsed, touching and rubbing together as he turned her. His manhood stroked her bare bottom, and his hands played over her breasts. Then he shut off the water and reached for a thick terry towel, drying her leisurely, rubbing the towel lightly between her legs while he watched her. He saw the searing longing in her brown eyes, and then she squeezed her eyes closed, her hands clutching his upper arms while she moaned with pleasure.

"Just a minute," he said, hurrying to get his billfold and get protection. He was back quickly and when he entered the bathroom, she was pulling on a white terry robe furnished by the hotel.

He put on the condom and then embraced her and pushed aside the robe.

As he kissed her, he picked her up. When she wrapped her long legs around him, he spread his feet to brace himself, lowering her body slowly on his swollen rod. He felt her surround him and knew he'd be unable to keep the control he had the first time. Her tongue flicked in his ear, driving him to thrust deeper.

"I want you to come again," he whispered. "I want to love you all night long and make you wild because of the way you respond to me," he added, and she turned her head to kiss him madly.

When he plunged again and again into her softness, she took him to paradise. He shook with satisfaction as he climaxed. She cried out with pleasure at the same time, reaching her own release.

He sagged back against the wall and in minutes let her slide to her feet.

"What you do to me is sinful," he whispered. "Deliciously sinful," he added. He stepped back into the shower, taking her with him, and they showered again, soaping each other.

"Do you think this is wise?" Lara asked. "We might not ever get out of this bathroom if we keep up this routine."

"There's nothing routine about it," he answered in a deep voice. He dropped a kiss on her shoulder before he gently soaped her. In minutes she stepped out to dry and put on her robe again and hurried to the sitting room.

He joined her in his robe, getting fresh glasses and pouring them chilled champagne to replace the almost untouched drinks he had poured earlier. He pulled out a chair, sat down and caught her wrist to draw her down on his lap.

"Now we can study the room service menu and decide what we want to order," he said, picking up a menu. She held one side while he held the other and they decided on steaks. Eli ordered, set down the phone and pushed open her robe.

"The cook said it'll be forty minutes before our dinner will be ready and delivered. I know how to make that time fly," Eli said, cupping her breast and caressing her nipple.

She inhaled, leaned forward as if she were going to kiss him, but then she halted only inches from his face. "You're insatiable."

"I think we both are," he replied. "And I love it." He wound his fingers in her hair and pulled her to him to kiss her while he felt her hands tugging at his robe to open it and explore him with her hands.

Eli thought he was hungry, but when their steak dinners came, after a few bites, all he wanted was to carry her back to bed. And he noticed her appetite was lagging, too. In minutes he gave up on food and stood to pull her into his arms.

It was a night of wild passion, but finally exhaustion was upon them. He pulled her close in his arms, relishing her softness, entangling his legs with hers. He dozed a moment and then stirred, stroking her silky hair that fell over his shoulder. "Lara," he murmured totally relaxed, barely able to put words together. "You've ruined me," he drawled.

"You loved it," she replied, and he chuckled, falling asleep.

Lara settled closer against him, tangling her fingers in his chest hair and smiling. She had loved every minute with him. What would tomorrow be like? She told herself not to expect him to pursue knowing her.

One-night stands weren't her style, yet from the way he had talked, they weren't his, either.

Soon enough she would know, she thought and snuggled close. His arm tightened around her and she twisted to look at him but saw he slept. Contented, she closed her eyes and drifted into dreams about Eli.

Lara awakened, momentarily disoriented as she stared at an unfamiliar ceiling. The bedroom was bathed in morning light.

Then she became aware of a warm body beside her. She turned to look at Eli. His arm was wrapped around her waist and he held her close against him. His leg was over hers. Locks of his brown hair tumbled over his forehead and his chest expanded with each deep breath.

Tantalizing, fantastic memories tumbled in on her. She wanted to lean down and brush a kiss across his mouth. She slipped out of bed and pulled on the white robe. As she did, she knocked Eli's billfold off the table. She bent to retrieve it. It had fallen open, and she realized that she had never learned Eli's full name. Last night passion had been paramount.

She glanced at his picture, looked at his name and froze.

Three

Lara leaned down to make certain she had read the name correctly. *Eli Ashton!* There it was in black-and-white and no doubt about it.

Aghast, she stared as the name *Ashton* leaped up at her.

When she looked back at the man sleeping in the bed, opposing emotions tore at her. He had been fantastic and appealing and sexy.

An Ashton! The last person on earth she would want to go out with, much less know on an intimate basis.

And now it all fell together so easily—why hadn't she seen it? She had been blinded by physical attraction that had overruled all else.

An Ashton! Tall, green eyes—but the world was filled with green-eyed people. She thought of Trace—brown hair, green eyes, but other than those two features, Eli and Trace hardly resembled each other.

Eli Ashton. She didn't know which Ashton family he belonged to—son, nephew, another family. It didn't matter which one of Spencer's offspring it was. Eli was an Ashton and she'd guess he was Spencer's son. He had the Ashton family traits—love of women, expecting to have his way, total confidence in himself.

Who was he? She knew Spencer had another wife before Lilah and he'd had children by her. A few months ago the news had broken that there had been a wife even before *that*, a first marriage to a woman in Nebraska that made the second marriage illegitimate. Which family did Eli belong to? The Nebraska Ashtons or the Ashtons who owned Louret Vineyards? Then she remembered that he was a winemaker.

Eli Ashton was from Louret Vineyards! Lara wanted to gnash her teeth, but she reassured herself that she wouldn't see him ever again. The two California Ashton families had nothing to do with each other.

Or they never had until recently. Her mother told her that two of Spencer's daughters from his earlier marriage had come to Ashton Estate to talk to Megan, Paige and Charlotte Ashton to make overtures of peace between the two families. Spencer's wife, Lilah, had thrown them out, so that probably had made the rift between the families even bigger.

Lara looked at him again, remembering the night and the passion, the intimacy between them. She was torn with conflicting emotions, hating that she had involved herself with an Ashton, yet at the same time unable to view the past hours with regret.

Panic gripped her. She had to get out of the hotel and away from him before he awakened.

Hastily, she gathered her things and rushed to the bathroom to dress. She fumbled with her clothes, yanking them on. How could she have gone off with a stranger the way she had? What had gotten into her to toss aside all common sense?

And the night of lust! She had been wanton and abandoned with a man who was a total stranger. She had never had a one-night stand with a man, much less one whose full name she didn't know.

Why had she thought it would be all right because she met him at the reception at the estate? It was only reasonable to expect the place to be crawling with Ashtons.

She held her breath and opened the door.

He was lying on his side, his arm thrown across the bed, and he didn't look as if he had moved since she had slipped out of his embrace. For one minute she was caught and held, her gaze roaming down the length of him while she remembered what it felt like to be in his arms. He was handsome in a rugged manner, far too appealing. Longing tugged at her, and she shook her head, shoving aside any yearning she might feel.

With her heart pounding, she crossed the suite and let herself out as quietly as possible.

She all but ran to the lobby to ask a bellman to get her a taxi. Within minutes she climbed into a cab and gave the driver directions. As the cab pulled away from the curb, she looked back at the hotel. Eli was in there asleep. She slammed shut that train of thought and turned her back on the hotel. She needed to put last night out of her mind. But she knew she would never forget Eli Ashton.

She would ask one of her friends, another of the housekeeping staff from Ashton Estate, to come pick her up. She didn't want to leave a trail behind that Eli could easily follow. If he even wanted to follow it. Once he knew her ties to his father's other family, he would lose all interest, she was certain. The Louret

Vineyard head winemaker would not pursue a maid from the Ashton Estate for more than one reason.

On the other hand, why wouldn't he want to see her? She had let him seduce her without the slightest protest. Far from it—she had been as eager and willing as he.

Why had she ever gotten involved with a man whose identity she didn't know?

If Eli searched for her—and she doubted he would—he couldn't find her without knowing her last name.

She had thought he was mourning Spencer's death. If he was a son Spencer had sired and abandoned, then his grim countenance had not been from sorrow but from fury. Lara realized that Eli had been hurting when he snapped at her on the veranda. She inhaled, trying to squelch the sympathy that stirred in her.

She sat back in the cab and closed her eyes. Eli Ashton. The appalling discovery of his identity still rocked her. She was shocked at her own behavior, astounded to learn who he was. The knowledge kept running through her mind over and over. And the knowledge that he may have been hurting badly yesterday nagged at her. Beneath all that rough exterior was a good man.

The cab dropped her in front of another hotel as she'd directed. She went inside and used the phone to call her closest friend, Franci Stanopolis, and asked her to come get her.

Once in Franci's ancient yellow car, Lara stared gloomily out the window while Franci's dark-brown eyes sparkled with curiosity.

"Well," Franci said, "are you going to tell me anything?"

"Yes, but you have to keep this one to yourself," Lara said and proceeded to tell brief highlights of how she had left the estate to go and have a drink with Eli.

"What's he look like? I'll bet he's handsome," Franci said eagerly.

"He's handsome and he took me to a restaurant in Napa and we talked. The time flew past. Franci, it was just an intense attraction—that's all I can say to explain it."

"Love at first sight."

"Hardly," Lara remarked dryly. "More like lust at first sight. He's handsome, wealthy, sexy."

"You're like Cinderella, except you don't have a glass slipper. Why do you look so glum? Did he walk out on you this morning?"

"I walked out on him."

Franci screeched, shooting a quick glance at her friend. "Why on earth would you do something like that? He sounds like Prince Charming!"

"Hardly. Franci, it sounds terrible now, but we didn't bother with last names. They just didn't come up. We talked about everything else under the sun."

"Ah, you hit it off in more ways than just physical. And I'll bet he's a great person."

"This morning I saw his open billfold. He's Eli Ashton."

"No! Which one of the other Ashtons is that? Spencer is beginning to turn up a harem of wives and children."

"Spencer liked women. So does Eli."

"You don't know that. All you know is that he liked one woman, a pretty redhead I know."

"He likes women. Believe me," Lara insisted.

"Which Ashton is he?"

"He's from Louret Vineyards. He said he is a winemaker so that rules out the Nebraska family that Spencer abandoned."

Franci glanced at her friend. "Why on earth did you walk out on him?"

"I can't believe you're asking that question. This is Spencer Ashton's son—you know how I loathed Spencer and his groping hands. Spencer made my life hell—yours, too, except he couldn't hold it over you that he would fire your mother if you didn't let him paw you," Lara said bitterly.

"That doesn't mean you hate his son or that his son is like him." Franci's black curls bobbed as she shook her head.

"To quote an old saying, 'The apple never falls far from the tree.'" She shivered. "I detested Spencer!"

"Don't let the police hear you say that one!" Franci exclaimed. "I still say you can't hold what Spencer did against his son. A son he didn't even raise. Trace isn't like that."

"No, he's not. Anyway, I'm out of Eli's league and, if he had learned I was an Ashton Estate domestic, he would have walked out on me."

"Only if he's a snob. Did you think he was a snob? And be honest."

"I don't care. For plenty of reasons the head winemaker of Louret Vineyards will not want to pursue getting to know a maid at the Ashton Estate. And you know how Lilah Ashton feels about that other family. She despises them and threw out those women from that family when they came on a peace mission recently. I just hope Lilah doesn't learn about this, because I wouldn't do anything to jeopardize Mom's job as head housekeeper."

"Lilah isn't going to fire your mother because you went out with one of those other Ashtons."

"You don't know that. Spencer threatened to fire people— and did—all the time."

"Lilah isn't Spencer. She might get in a huff, but she won't fire your mom for something you did. Besides, your mom is excellent at her job. Lilah isn't going to get rid of someone who does such a super job. Your mom or you."

"I hope you're right," Lara said.

"Tell me more about him. Is he a sexy kisser?"

"Franci! That's off-limits."

"I'm not asking intimate details, just is he a sexy kisser. On a scale of one to ten, where does he rate?"

"About one hundred," Lara answered dryly.

"Oh, my. Maybe you should rethink not seeing him again."

"Franci, he won't want to see me, a lowly maid. And I'll be back in law school again in the fall. Besides, I don't want to get involved with Spencer Ashton's son. And I've told you before, until I'm out of school, I definitely don't want a man complicating my life."

"Was Eli Ashton at all like Spencer last night?"

"Yes. He gets his way. He's very determined."

"That's not bad as long as he doesn't hurt anyone. Has he hurt people the way Spencer did?"

"I'm sure he hasn't," Lara admitted with a sigh. "When he mentioned his family, his voice was warm and his remarks were complimentary. Eli may not be like his father, but it doesn't matter. Our lives are not in the same world."

"You just like being in control. Maybe when you meet a man who also likes to be in control, it's dynamite."

Lara took a deep breath and stared out the car window. It had been dynamite, all right.

When she was finally home again, she hurried upstairs to her room. Each step she took, climbing to the second floor and then going higher to the third floor and the servants' quarters, took her farther from Eli's world of luxury.

She stepped into her small, yellow and white bedroom, closing the door and flinging down her purse. She went across the room, pulling off her black dress and balling it up, tossing it on the floor of the closet. In the bathroom she yanked off her plain cotton panties that should have given Eli a clue to her status. She tried to forget their loving yet she was unable to banish images of Eli—virile, naked, his hands creating ecstasy.

But despite what they had shared together, Eli was an Ashton and the Ashtons were not to be trifled with. In fairness, she had to admit that Trace, Megan and Paige were fine, likable people. Blood ties to Spencer hadn't turned them into monsters. It was Spencer who was the monster. Eli probably viewed Spencer as a monster, too.

But good or bad, Eli represented wealth and privilege and a world that she was not privy to.

She sighed and shook her head. "I simply refuse to think about you, Eli Ashton," she declared loudly in the shower.

She dressed in her black maid's uniform to begin her duties at the estate. As she wound her hair behind her head, she wondered what Eli would think if he could see her now.

Eli stirred and stretched and rolled over, running his arm over the cool sheets. He opened his eyes and then sat up to gaze around.

"Lara?" he called. When she didn't answer, the first inkling that something was amiss struck him and he swung his feet out of bed and stood.

Four

"Lara!" he called again, and still there was only silence.

"Dammit," he grumbled, going to the bathroom to grab a towel to wrap around his waist. He walked through the suite and then called the front desk, but a new clerk had come on, and no one knew anything about Lara.

Eli raked his fingers through his hair and searched the suite more carefully. With every passing minute his aggravation increased.

Lara had left without a trace. No note, no phone number—nothing. Lara who? He realized that he didn't know her last name. He hadn't particularly wanted to give his yesterday, but he should have gotten her full name.

He was disappointed, hurt and annoyed at himself. Today he had expected to exchange phone numbers, learn where she lived and tell her where he lived. He had expected to wake up and make love to her again. He would have had room service deliver breakfast and maybe he could have talked her into staying with him through the morning.

For a few minutes he was lost in remembering their moments of lovemaking and her wild responses to him. He became hot and aroused just thinking about her lush body and how her hands had played over him.

In frustration he raked his fingers through his thick hair again and swore quietly. Anger churned in him and made him want to forget her and go on home, but he couldn't. He wanted to see her.

Why had she just walked out on him? They had fallen asleep in each other's arms, and she had seemed warm and caring— not the type to just vanish without a word.

She was an acquaintance of Spencer's other family—she'd been at his funeral reception. But he couldn't expect any information about her from them. They wouldn't give him the time of day. Lara. That's all he knew about her name. But it wasn't all he knew about her. They'd had a firestorm of lovemaking last night.

From the very first few words they had exchanged, she had intrigued and attracted him. Everywhere he looked in the suite, he could see her in his imagination. He remembered everything about her, her kisses, how her hair sprang back into curls when he combed his fingers through it, her flirtatious brown eyes. Her fantastic long legs. Her kisses that set him on fire with a mere memory.

He swore softly. It wasn't going to help him any to stand around in the empty hotel suite and think about the night. He called room service, ordered breakfast and then headed for the bathroom to shower.

He drank a glass of orange juice, but his appetite had fled. Getting dressed in his rumpled shirt and trousers, he went to the lobby to check out. He made inquiries and tipped people and found a valet who had helped her into a cab.

No danger of anyone not noticing her or forgetting her, he knew. She was a beautiful woman, and it was easy to find someone who remembered her.

Eli checked out, got in his car and headed north. He called the vineyard and talked briefly to his brother Cole and said he was on his way home. All the time he talked, as he drove through Napa, he found himself looking for Lara, watching other cars, looking at people walking past on the street.

One minute he swore he would find her. Then the next minute he told himself to forget her. But forgetting her was impossible; he wanted to be with her right now.

He picked up his cell phone, called information for the number of the cab company and then tried to locate the driver who had driven her away from the hotel.

A dispatcher said he would find the driver and get back to Eli. After thanking the man, Eli broke the connection and tossed the phone on the car seat beside him in disgust. Let her go, he told himself. It was another disappointment like so many he'd had before.

His thoughts jumped to Spencer. Soon there would be a reading of the will. Would Spencer finally right some of the wrongs he had committed in his life?

Eli wondered if the police would ever catch the person who had murdered Spencer. If there were any clues, the police were keeping quiet about them. They had talked to him the day after the murder, but that didn't surprise Eli. It was well-known that he had no kind feelings for Spencer. But he and Spencer also hadn't crossed paths often, except for wine events—times when Louret labels had been given higher acclaim than wines from the Ashton vineyards.

How Eli had enjoyed every triumph that Louret wines had had over Ashton Estate wines. He guessed each award had infuriated Spencer. He hoped they had.

While Louret couldn't produce the quantity of Ashton Estate vineyards, Louret always topped Ashton in quality. Their boutique winery was small but superior, and Eli was proud of his part in the achievement of excellence, and he was proud of his mother for all she had done.

As he left town he thought about how his whole family had pulled together through the years and what a fine job they had done. His brother, Cole, was indispensable and his baby sister, Jillian, was becoming an expert. It amazed him how capable she had become and she was still learning. Of course, they were butting heads over some of her ideas. Little, stubborn "Shrimp" wouldn't give up on her vision for a *meritage*—softening the Cabernet Sauvignon with other varieties. Maybe he should listen to her.

His sister Mercedes surprised and pleased him, too, with her marketing skills. Mason, the youngest, was studying in France, and his knowledge should help them develop more superior wines. Together they were all building a premier boutique winery that rivaled some of the elite wineries of Europe.

As Eli sped north along the highway, unbidden, memories crowded out all thoughts of Louret wines. He could remember Lara's perfume, her laughter, her kisses. Why had she slipped away without letting him know?

He wasn't accustomed to being brushed off by women, much less one he had become intimate with. He knew nothing about her or where to start looking.

To hell with searching for her, he thought. If she wanted out of his life, fine. He could forget her. The world was filled with beautiful women. He'd get back to Louret and throw himself into work and forget her, he told himself. Yet even as he promised himself to stop thinking about her, he could envision her brown eyes and her smile.

He tried to remember his schedule for today. Yesterday he had cleared everything off his calendar because of the funeral.

He remembered that he was going to check on their oldest small oak barrels to see what needed to be replaced. Also, they were getting new white-oak barrels, which he preferred for maturing Syrah. Those were the best barrels to create a slow oxidation of the wine to give it the finest complexity of aroma.

He sped north through Napa up Highway 29 until he reached The Vines, the family estate. He turned onto the winding road and when the French country–style house came into view, he thought how much more charming it was, though not as large and elegant as the Ashton Estate mansion.

Sunshine splashed over the dark-gray slate roofs and bathed the gray and white rustic stone in warm light. Dark-green shutters flanked the downstairs mullioned windows. Bright green vines winding on trellises gave the home an old-world charm. Usually the sight of the house showered a glow of satisfaction on him, but today he couldn't shake his disappointment and annoyance over Lara's disappearance.

He strode inside through the pale-blue foyer, his heels scraping the bare wood floors.

His mother, Caroline, was just heading into the family room. Dressed in pale-yellow linen slacks and a matching blouse, she looked stylish and regal, and Eli crossed the hall to brush a kiss on her cheek.

Caroline held eighteen-month-old Jack Sheridan in her arms. Eli tried to banish thoughts of Spencer when he looked at Spencer's illegitimate offspring. Little Jack had been as tossed aside by Spencer as Eli and his family had.

The chubby-cheeked baby was cute and the whole family loved him. Jack held out a small stuffed bear to Eli. "Baya," he said.

"I see the bear," Eli answered, ruffling Jack's red hair. "He's a cutie," he said to Caroline. "Where's Anna?"

"I told her I'd watch Jack for a while and give her a little break. He's adorable, Eli. And he has a new word—he can say *light* now."

"Anna's an angel for taking in her nephew to raise. And you're an angel for giving them a home and security."

"You would have done the same thing. Imagine! Her sister dying and leaving a baby all alone. And now the press is hounding Anna, and she's getting threatening phone calls—Anna just needed shelter from the storm." Caroline looked at the little boy in her arms. "Anna's a strong woman—she'll get along and Jack is just precious. They can stay forever as far as I'm concerned."

"You'll get so attached to Jack, he'll be like one of your own. Watch out you don't get a broken heart. Someday Anna will leave."

"I know, but hopefully, she'll let us all continue to be part of their lives." Caroline eyed Eli and her eyebrows arched. "You look like you fell out of the car, Eli. I hate to say I told you so, but I knew going to the funeral reception would be rough."

"I'm all right, Mom," he said. "Seeing all of them just made me all the more proud of you and Dad and our family. We've done all right."

"That we have, thanks in large part to you."

He shook his head. "Dad taught us well," Eli said, referring to Lucas Shepherd, his stepfather. "We're all a competent team."

She smiled up at him. "You so rarely take a day off, then to spend it at *Spencer's* funeral…" Her voice faded away and she shook her head. "I don't want to see the house again."

"I like ours better," he said, walking away from her. "It's cozier. Mom, I still want you to give some thought to letting our attorney see if Ashton Estate is yours now. Spencer wasn't legally married to you, because he never divorced his first wife in Nebraska, so to my way of thinking, he couldn't inherit from Granddad."

"We've been over that, Eli. I don't want the bitter fight we'd have on our hands if we pursued it. It would only lead to unhappiness. You've got a satisfying life. You don't need that battle."

"Sorry to worry you. I just want you to think about it and talk to Dad about it."

"Lucas feels the same as I do, but I'll think about it a little more. You take care of yourself, Eli," she said, an uncustomary caution before she turned and disappeared into the family room while he wondered why she had said that to him. He could hear her talking to Jack and Jack babbling in return. Eli shook his head. That baby would have all their hearts before long.

Forgetting about Jack, Eli took the stairs two at a time to his suite, striding through the wide hall with a glance at the family photos adorning the walls, thankful that his mother had The Vines. At the back of the house he had his own suite, including a living room and kitchenette. He walked through the living room with its blue and green decor. The large oil painting over his mantel was an accurate picture of the Louret vineyards in summer.

He tossed his coat on a chair in his bedroom, where the colors were an extension of those in his living room. He got out a fresh shirt and trousers, pulling on a pale-gray sport shirt and gray cotton slacks. He combed his hair and tried to keep from thinking about Lara, hoping to immerse himself in work.

The cab company called him back a few moments later. They had found the driver who had picked up Lara. The man would return to the office in an hour. Eli thanked the dispatcher and replaced the receiver.

Stepping outside, he left for the office. Beneath peaked roofs, the two-story winery had offices on the upper floor, the tasting room on the ground floor. The warm, sunny June day should have lifted his spirits, but he knew he was in a dark mood and that he needed to snap out of it.

Eli glanced at the vineyards and saw his half brother Grant looking at the vines and talking to Henry Lydell, Louret's new foreman who had replaced Russ Gannon. Russ had fallen in love and married Grant's niece Abigail from Nebraska a few months ago. Eli liked Grant and experienced a connection with the Nebraska farmer. They both were men of the earth, Grant the farmer and Eli the winemaker. It was a bond that was forged almost the first day Grant was at their house.

Eli thought about the shock of Grant's revelation that Spencer had had a wife in Nebraska he had never divorced and Grant and his sister were children of that marriage. Eli wondered who had received the greatest shock—Grant at forty-three to discover his father was still alive and had walked out on them, or all the other Ashtons to learn of another marriage of Spencer's. When he had been turned away by Lilah and Spencer, Caroline had invited Grant to stay at Louret.

The news had been a bomb when the press got hold of it. The tabloids had carried bold, lurid headlines, especially after it was revealed that Spencer had never divorced his first wife.

Eli entered the winery. For the next two hours he worked,

checking on the barrels, talking to Cole, walking blocks of the vineyards to look at the grapes and checking on the thinning of the canopy of green leaves so that the right amount of sunlight reached the clusters of grapes.

Shortly after three o'clock, Eli stopped work and left. Telling himself he was every kind of a fool, he got in his car and sped back to the cab company in Napa. It took only a few minutes to talk to the driver who had picked up Lara. He had deposited her at the Regency and the last he had seen of her, she had started into the hotel. Thanking the driver, Eli pulled out his wallet and gave the man payment for his information. At the Regency Eli ran into a dead end with no trace of her.

Eli drove home in a darker mood than before. She had gone to a hotel. Was she an Ashton relative who had flown in for the funeral and had stayed at a hotel in the city? A friend of the family? A call girl? The last he didn't want to consider, yet she was beautiful enough, kept things impersonal, and no telling who Spencer had known or been involved with.

Eli hit the steering wheel with the palm of his hand and swore, annoyed with himself for pursuing the matter. He clamped his jaw closed, and got his mind back on the vineyard.

It was early summer and the vines were doing well. Louret grew Pinot Noir, Merlot, Cabernet Sauvignon and Petite Verdot grapes. Their Caroline Chardonnay was gaining great reviews. At this stage of the summer, they had had inflorescence. The new shoots had blossomed and were about to transform into tiny green grapes that would ripen during lazy summer days until the fall harvest.

He could remember Lara sipping the glass of Caroline Chardonnay that he had ordered. He shook his head. "Get out of my thoughts," he said quietly.

* * *

Back at his office, Eli found a note lying on the desk. He picked it up to see that he'd had four calls: three from business-men he knew and they involved the winery or the vineyard. The fourth was from a stranger: Stephen Cassidy, Attorney at Law.

Eli dialed the number and got voice mail. When he called the cell number, a man answered, identifying himself as Stephen Cassidy.

"Mr. Cassidy, I'm Eli Ashton and I'm returning your call," Eli said.

He listened to the deep voice. "Mr. Ashton, I was Spencer Ashton's attorney. He had his affairs in order, and we can get right to the reading of Spencer's will. I have to notify everyone mentioned in the will, and when I talked with your mother she said I should call you."

"That's fine," Eli replied. "I'll represent my family."

"Excellent. I've set a date for the reading next Monday morn-ing, the thirteenth of June. For the family's benefit, we've made arrangements to meet at the Ashton Estate at ten o'clock. Will you be able to attend?"

"I'll be there," Eli promised and listened as the attorney told him goodbye. Eli replaced the receiver, wondering again if Spen-cer had made amends in his will.

Eli went to the vineyards to do some pruning and check for powdery or downy mildew. He snapped off suckers and in-spected the tiny clusters of grapes that were forming. Even as he worked with the vines, his mind wandered back to Lara.

The rest of the week he failed to get her out of his mind. He made no effort to find her, but his family noticed his brooding. All of them chalked it up to tension over the reading of Spen-cer's will.

Monday finally came, and Eli dressed in a navy suit with a red tie. Driving up to the Ashton Estate for the second time in his life, he tried to keep out memories of meeting Lara at the funeral reception.

He rang the chimes, and a maid swung open the door to usher him through a large elegant foyer. They climbed four steps to a secondary foyer, and she motioned to an open door on the left.

"In the library, sir," she said politely, and was gone.

He entered the library, where people had already gathered. Folding chairs had been set up facing a massive desk. Eli noticed the sharp looks he received from the other Ashtons, none of whom came forward to greet him. He took a seat at the end of the row, leaving half a row of empty seats between him and Lilah Ashton.

Eli glanced around the library while bitterness welled up in him. The library was Spencer's domain. On the desk in a gold frame was a picture, turned slightly, and Eli could see the Ashton family, including Spencer. An oil portrait of Spencer hung on one wall. Bookshelves lined other walls, and even though it was a different library, the room brought back sharp memories of Eli's childhood and that stormy night when he had overheard Spencer tell Caroline he was leaving her and the children.

The tall attorney with his salt-and-pepper hair looked natty in a gray suit. He walked up to Eli and extended his hand. "I'm Stephen Cassidy," he announced.

"Eli Ashton," Eli said, standing and shaking the man's hand.

"Will others from your family be here?"

"No, I'm representing them."

"Fine." Stephen Cassidy turned as another man joined them. "Mr. Ashton, this is my assistant, Ty Koenig."

Eli shook hands with a stocky, black-haired man who smiled and gazed at him through thick glasses.

"We're all here and we'll start in just a few," Ty Koenig said. "Just have a seat."

"Thanks," Eli said, and sat as the two men walked away. Harsh looks were directed Eli's way, and he clamped his jaw closed while his anger mounted. Once again, viewing the house, the knowledge that Spencer had stolen all of this from his mother was a knife in Eli's heart. Eli hated being here as much as he hated the other Ashtons, but the attorney had called him, so he and his family were in Spencer's will. He remembered the argument he'd had with Cole when he told him about the call the next morning. Cole had stopped in Eli's office to give him a note from Mrs. McKillup, their bookkeeper.

Cole's green eyes had blazed with anger and he'd lowered the clipboard he held in his hands. Trotting after Cole was his dog, Tillie, a greyhound-Dalmatian mix. At the sight of Eli, Tillie wagged her tail and flopped down on the floor beside Cole.

"You're crazy to go," Cole snapped. "The attorney will have to give us a copy of the will whether or not we attend. It isn't like a contest where you have to be present to win."

"I'm going. I can represent the family, since no one else wants to set foot on the place."

"Damn straight, no one wants to," Cole said. "They don't want us there, either. I don't want to look at the Ashton Estate and think about what Spencer did to Mom. You'll regret going."

"Maybe I will, but I still intend to be there. Trace and Walker Ashton can't scare me away."

"They don't scare me. I just think I might take a swing at them. And if I might, you're going to."

"I'll control my temper."

"Yeah, right."

"I will. But I might not this morning if you keep it up," Eli grumbled, and Cole grinned, turning to hurry away. After he had widened the distance between them, at the door of Eli's office, he looked over his shoulder. "You can take Tillie for protection."

"Dixie's cat, Hulk, maybe, but never your wimp of a dog," Eli said, referring to Cole's wife's unusually brave pet. Cole's grin widened.

Now he was here at Ashton Estate and, so far, controlling himself just fine, but he'd be glad when this morning was over and done.

Seated in a cluster along the row of chairs were the other Ashtons. Eli glanced at Lilah Ashton and her children. Eli had occasionally seen Lilah Ashton. He had to admit that she was an attractive woman, one whose looks, he was certain, had been enhanced by Spencer's money. Black became her. Her chic, chin-length red hair was set off by her black dress. Next to her, in a flawless brown suit, sat Eli's cousin—Spencer's tall, black-haired nephew, Walker Ashton—who had been raised like Spencer's own son and now was the executive vice president of Ashton-Lattimer Corporation. The chair to Lilah Ashton's left was empty, but Trace Ashton stood a few feet away talking to his younger sister, Paige Ashton. Dressed in a gray suit, Trace was tall and lean and looked physically fit. His sister was shorter. Eli knew Paige Ashton was the event planner for the Ashton Estate. Her smiling picture had been on brochures and in wine magazines.

Beside Walker Ashton was his sister, Charlotte, Spencer's niece. Like her brother, her Native American heritage showed in her straight black hair. Eli wondered about Charlotte and Walker. Word was, that after all these years since Spencer had taken them in to raise after his brother's death, he had told them that their mother had also died. Now, according to rumors, Spencer's duplicity had been revealed when Charlotte had heard that their mother was alive. If that turned out to be the truth, Eli thought, it would be just one more evil perpetrated by Spencer. One more scandal to rock the family and feed the tabloids.

Taking a seat to the right of Charlotte was Megan Ashton, now married. Beside her was her new husband, Simon Pearce.

While Eli waited, he watched Stephen Cassidy take the empty seat beside Lilah Ashton, talking to her and patting her shoulder. For another five minutes the attorney conversed with her, this time putting his arm around her shoulders. Eli noticed the lawyer seemed unduly interested in her. Was more scandal going to rock the Ashtons? Eli wondered idly. Or was the attorney simply being attentive to the grieving widow?

Finally clearing his throat, Cassidy began the reading. He talked briefly about the gathering for the reading of Spencer's will and then he began: "I, Spencer Winston Ashton, being of sound mind…"

Eli listened, looking at the people nearby. He had cousins and half brothers and half sisters present, yet they didn't speak and they were almost total strangers. The world of wine was the only common ground that brought them into contact occasionally, but even there they gave each other a wide berth.

Jerking his attention back to the will, Eli listened attentively as Stephen Cassidy read: "I hereby bequeath my shares of Ashton-Lattimer stock to Walker Ashton."

Hot anger exploded in Eli, and he clenched his fists while he fought to keep his expression impassive and to sit still. Spencer left Walker, a nephew, his shares of Ashton-Lattimer Corporation, Eli's grandfather's company. Spencer was a bastard. Eli wondered why he had expected anything decent from Spencer. With an effort, Eli pulled his concentration back to Stephen Cassidy as he continued to read:

"To Charlotte Ashton, I bequeath the sum of twenty thousand dollars."

Eli glanced at her. She stared straight ahead and not a flicker of emotion showed in her expression, but she had to be disappointed or angry or hurt. Twenty thousand from Spencer was a paltry sum when all of his wealth and vast estate were taken into consideration. Compared to the stock shares that her brother received, the money was nothing.

Eli suspected that Spencer hadn't righted any wrongs he had done in the past, and Eli knew that would include his own family. Yet Cassidy had called him to hear the will, so there had to be some mention of Caroline and her family.

"To my beloved wife, Lilah Ashton and our three children, Trace, Paige and Megan Ashton, I leave my property which includes the Ashton Estate house and vineyards, the winery, all monies in my accounts, any savings and stocks aside from Ashton-Lattimer Corporation shares of stock. This property and holdings are to be divided equally in order that my family will share—"

Eli listened to the words, each bequest another punch to his gut. Caroline and her family had been cut out of the will just as Spencer had cut his family out of his life. Grant and little Jack hadn't been acknowledged, either. Nor had Spencer's two Nebraska grandchildren, Ford and Abigail, who had been taken in to be raised by Grant Ashton. Eli clenched his jaw, resolving to push his family to contest the will and to try to get back the Ashton holdings for his mother. Spencer hadn't deserved all that he'd ruthlessly taken. It would mean another Ashton scandal but one that Eli welcomed.

"To Caroline Ashton and each of her children—Eli Ashton, Cole Ashton, Mercedes Ashton and Jillian Ashton, I hereby bequeath the sum of one dollar each."

Eli's ears buzzed and his pulse drummed with fury. Cole had warned him that he was foolish to even go to the reading of the will, yet Caroline agreed with Eli that someone should represent the family. Cole had been right.

Hot and angry, Eli didn't hear the rest of the will. The walls of the room seemed to close in. He couldn't wait to get out and leave the estate and the Ashtons that Spencer had claimed as his family.

Finally Stephen Cassidy was finished and immediately back at Lilah Ashton's side. Eli started toward the door and almost collided with Walker Ashton.

"Did you actually expect him to bequeath anything to you?" Walker asked, blocking Eli's way. The animosity flowing between them was tangible. Eli fought to control his temper and his fists.

"Now you own the shares of my grandfather's business," Eli said bitterly, jamming his fists into his trouser pockets.

"They were my uncle's shares of stock," Walker snapped back, his brown eyes flashing with anger. "And he's left the shares to me. He wanted me to have them. If I recall the circumstances, your grandfather willed the Ashton-Lattimer shares to Spencer."

"He trusted Spencer and didn't realize what a deceitful snake the man was."

"Spencer was no snake," Walker snarled, visibly bristling as his face flushed. "You saw the hundreds of friends gathered for his funeral. Your grandfather left everything to Spencer because he wanted Spencer to have it all. Not your mother but Spencer," Walker reminded him.

Eli turned to stride away, knowing if he didn't get distance between them, he would resort to blows. He took two steps and faced Trace Ashton who had been talking to one of his sisters. Trace's green eyes were cold and his jaw set as he faced Eli.

"You need to get off this property," Trace said. "You weren't welcome here when Spencer was alive, and that hasn't changed now that he's gone. If he were here, he'd throw you off himself because your presence upsets my mother."

Eli clenched his fists again. "It's your property, but you know Spencer stole it from my mother. At one time this was all my grandfather's."

"My father didn't steal anything. It was given to him by your grandfather. Go back to your little vineyard."

"It's a damn fine vineyard whether it's small or not. We beat your wines in any competition."

"Get the hell out of here, Eli, before I throw you out."

"Don't worry. I was on my way. I can't get away from here fast enough." Eli ground out the words and brushed past Trace. Burning with rage, he fought the urge to take a swing at the younger Ashton.

Taking his hands from his pockets, Eli strode through the door, leaving the library and heading for the front entrance. At the top of the four steps into the lower foyer, he glanced back over his shoulder, half expecting Trace Ashton to follow him to see if he was leaving and half hoping Trace would. Eli would like to vent his pent-up anger and take a swing at Trace, but he wasn't going to be the one to throw the first punch.

When he looked back over his shoulder, he was immobilized. Was it his imagination playing tricks on him, or had he just seen Lara disappearing through an open door off the foyer?

Eli turned and strode back. The woman had been in a maid's uniform. Then he remembered the first time she had spoken to him on the veranda at the funeral reception. She had asked if she could get anything for him. He should have guessed, except she hadn't been in a maid's uniform then.

His pulse sped up as he stopped in the open door of a formal dining room. He barely saw the long, polished table and side chairs, the sparkling crystal chandelier, the breakfront with priceless antiques. The only thing he really saw was Lara.

She stood across the room from him, setting a silver tea service on a credenza. She wore a black uniform with a white apron tied around her waist. Her thick hair was fastened in a bun behind her head. Even with the plain uniform, hairdo and black oxfords, she made his pulse race and stirred erotic images.

He stepped inside the dining room and closed the door.

Five

When Lara heard the door close, she turned around. Her heart missed a beat as she met Eli Ashton's stormy gaze. "What are you doing here?"

"Finding you," he said. His eyes glinted with fire when he crossed the room, stalking her like a panther. "Although you made it clear you didn't want to see me again."

Trying to ignore her racing pulse, she raised her chin. He was as handsome and appealing as she had remembered. "I mean, why are you at this house?" she asked.

"They had the reading of the will," he said, his voice fierce with rage.

"Oh, of course!" she exclaimed, feeling ridiculous. Yet she had never thought about Eli being included in Spencer's will. While Eli closed the distance between them, her mouth went dry and heat coiled in her, memories of his lovemaking assailing her.

Even angry, he still set her heart pounding. A few more feet closer, and he would hear it for himself.

When he stopped inches away, she could detect his familiar aftershave. In a navy suit, he was devastating, and it was impossible to keep her gaze from skimming over his features.

"You ran out on me."

"I found out you were an Ashton," she snapped back. "That's enough reason to run." She hated her intense reaction to seeing him again, but she couldn't control herself. "You're Spencer's son."

"Don't ever lump me with him! I'm not anything like that bastard," Eli retorted, a muscle working in his jaw, and she realized he was furious with Lilah's family.

"You're his son. You look like him. You act—"

"Don't say it," he ordered. His hand closed on her shoulder, and the glacial chill in his eyes stopped her. "I'm not like him. I hope to heaven I don't look like him."

"It's your green eyes. Those green eyes are a dominant trait," she said. "All the Ashtons have green eyes. It doesn't matter. I'm glad he's gone. I don't want any part of the Ashtons," she said, momentarily remembering Spencer and his roaming hands.

"It looks like to me you already have a large part of this family daily since you work here and you live here. It's a free world. There are a lot of other jobs, but you chose this one."

"I grew up here because my mother is the head housekeeper. I've stayed because of her."

"I looked for you," Eli said, pushing open his coat and jamming his hand on his hip. His stance was almost intimidating, except he was too magnetic. She had no intention of allowing him to get emotionally close to her again. "I never would have thought to look here. You know I'm Eli Ashton. I want to know who you are. What's your last name?"

"Hunter," she replied, fighting to avoid letting her gaze drift down over him.

"Well, Lara Hunter, I plan to get to know you a whole lot better."

"Why would you want to? We're like fire and ice. One will destroy the other."

"A better comparison would be fire and dynamite," he said, lowering his voice to a cajoling tone. A muscle still worked in his jaw, and his color was heightened, but his voice had changed and the wrath had gone from the depths of his eyes. "The chemistry we had was spectacular," he added.

"You're talking about sex."

"Damn straight. Making love with you was fantastic."

"And so you want a repeat of that night? No, thanks," she replied in what she hoped was a haughty tone that would bring him down a notch. "And I've told you why. Besides, it's impossible for me to go anywhere with you," she said, raising her chin.

"Of course it's possible," he said, moving closer and studying her intently. "That night, there wasn't all this antagonism between us."

"That's because I didn't dream I was with an Ashton."

"Look, I'm not like Spencer," he repeated tightly with a tone of steel returning to his voice. "Lucas Sheppard is the man who raised me and the man I claim as my father. My whole family is not like this bunch of Ashtons."

"I find that difficult to believe," she said, her fury surging over his resolve to get her to do what he wanted. "You have Spencer's blood in your veins, and you're as strong willed as he was. This conversation is proof."

"You're strong willed yourself, but that doesn't mean you take after Spencer," he shot back at her. He reached out, smoothing her already flat collar. Tingles diffused from his warm fingers brushing against her collarbone and throat. Still torn between fury and attraction, she tried to ignore the reaction she was having to him.

"Spencer remembered you in his will," she remarked. "You wouldn't be here otherwise," she said, to steer the conversation away from her.

He dropped his hands to his sides and clenched his fists, clamping his jaw closed and gazing beyond her. "He gave me the same he gave my mother and my siblings—exactly one dollar to each of us."

"A dollar!" she exclaimed, momentarily forgetting her ire and seeing why Eli was so incensed. She realized that along with his anger, he had to be hurting.

"I want to see you again because I know what you were like before you connected me with Spencer. Go to dinner with me tonight."

She thought of Spencer's groping hands and his open threats to fire her mother if Lara rejected his advances. Loathing curled in her at the mere thought of Spencer, and as long as she thought about the father, she knew she would be able to deal with his son.

"I'm not getting to know you or any other Ashton better. And even if I wanted to go out with you—which I don't—I can't because of my job."

"Why on earth not?" he asked. "This family doesn't own your soul."

"What I do can jeopardize my mother's job as well as mine."

"That's a joke! Because of Spencer's infamous transgressions, Lilah Ashton's family is steeped in scandal and ours hasn't gone untouched, either. We thought we were Spencer's first family, but we aren't. There was a wife in Nebraska whom he didn't divorce, so he committed bigamy with my mother. How the media gloried in that scandal! Spencer's affairs were common knowledge. Now it's come out that he had an illegitimate child. In the next few days, maybe even tonight, the media will make public the will and that my family once again was snubbed by Spencer. Spencer's been murdered and they don't know who did it. The list goes on and on. Who knows what new scandal will break tomorrow! This family can't fault you for dating one of the outcast Ashtons," he said, and she realized his bitterness and hurt ran deep. She knew Eli had to have been just a little boy when Spencer walked out on him and his family. It had to have left permanent scars.

A straight lock of brown hair fell on his forehead, and Lara fought the temptation to push it back in place. Her reaction to him heightened her annoyance.

"I can't believe they would fire their head housekeeper because her daughter went out with one of the other Ashtons," he continued. "Besides, how will they even know? We can go farther afield than Napa. It's a short drive to San Francisco and we can eat dinner there tonight."

"Are you listening to me?" she said, her indignation rising. "This is how you're exactly like your father!" she exclaimed, the sympathy she had briefly felt evaporating.

"Just stop right there," he demanded with a flash of fire in his eyes. "I know what I want and I go after it, but I'll say it again and again until I don't have to—I'm not like Spencer Ashton."

"We're at an impasse!" she exclaimed. She had raised her voice and leaned toward him. She had spent a lifetime exerting emotional control, but from the start, Eli could provoke her into losing that reserve. He leaned closer to her. Both of them were breathing hard, with mere inches separating them. Their gazes were locked, and the proximity was volatile. In spite of all the wrath bound up inside her, she longed to be in his arms and she wanted to kiss him. Anger morphed into desire that was spontaneous combustion.

As Eli hauled her against him, his mouth came down on hers, demanding and possessive. Her insides clenched. She stood on tiptoe, wound her arms around his neck and let her fury and desire pour out in a passionate kiss.

As craving banished fury, she thrust her hips against him.

Memories of their night of lust assailed her. She had vowed never to kiss him again or go out with him or even talk to him, but here she was, doing as he ordered and kissing him blindly— and savoring every moment of it.

Dimly, in the back of her mind, she realized she should stop. If Trace Ashton walked in on them, he would probably fire her on the spot because of the bad feeling between the two families. The knowledge hovered in her thoughts like fog, but she continued to kiss Eli, winding her fingers in his hair.

She finally pushed against him. "No!" she said, stepping out of his arms. "We can't kiss here."

"I agree this isn't the best of spots," Eli said, and his voice was husky, all the rage in his gaze had transformed to such scalding hunger that her pulse drummed.

"Even if you aren't exactly like Spencer and even if Lilah doesn't object, it won't work for us to see each other for another reason," Lara stated, trying to keep her wits about her. "Your world is vastly different from mine," she reminded him. "People like you don't socialize with people like me."

"To hell with that. You make this sound feudal." He draped

his hand on her shoulder. "Lara, I want to see you again. I want to take you to dinner where we can talk. If Trace Ashton finds me in here, there may be a fistfight, but I'm not budging until you accept my invitation."

"No. It's just unthinkable," she said. "Eli, it won't work, and I'm not—"

"Shh. I'll pick you up here about seven." He leaned closer. "I can be persistent." He placed his hand on her throat. His fingers were warm, and she could see satisfaction light his eyes. "Your pulse is racing, so your hesitation isn't because you don't like me or find me obnoxious. That's not it, is it?"

"You know it's not!" she exclaimed in exasperation. "I've been giving you my reasons for avoiding you since you walked into this room."

"None of which are valid," he said with that maddening perseverance that indicated he was going to continue until he got his way.

She bristled, yet in fairness, she knew that beneath that rough exterior, the man she had spent a passionate night with had also been considerate. She knew he was hurting over Spencer's dealings, and she hadn't helped his feelings by accusing him of being like his father. He was too fine a person for that. She gave a shake of her head, knowing she had come around.

"If you insist, let me meet you somewhere," she said as she capitulated.

"Fine. How about seven o'clock tonight? Same restaurant as last week."

"This is against my better judgment," she stated darkly.

"Your heart gives me a different answer. Want to see if my pulse is racing, too?"

"No, I don't!" she snapped, and saw amusement light his eyes.

"I can promise you that it is." He was only inches away, and then he leaned closer and his mouth covered hers again.

One more time he had caught her off guard. Her hands flew to grasp his upper arms as he leaned over her. She intended to push against him, horrified that he would continue to risk kissing her here in the Ashton mansion. Instead, her only conscious thought was that she desperately wanted to return his passionate kiss.

As his tongue thrust deep, her pulse thundered. Slowly he explored her mouth, demanding a response, making her his in too many ways. This strong-willed male would be her undoing. With desire kindling low in her, she returned his kiss.

He released her, running his fingers along her throat in a feathery caress.

"Thank heaven I found you," he said in a raspy voice.

"It may be disastrous," she whispered, wanting to step right back into his arms.

"Until tonight, Lara," he said, and turned to leave the room. At the door he looked back at her, and she realized she hadn't moved. She clamped her lips closed, lips that still tingled from his kiss, aware that her racing pulse hadn't slowed.

As soon as he left the room, she inhaled deeply and followed him out. When the front door closed behind him, she hurried to a window. A tough man, Eli Ashton stormed through life getting what he wanted. Except for Spencer—he'd never gotten his father's love. Momentarily she wondered about the murderer. Eli had enough rage and was strong enough, but his basic goodness had shone through that first night. Today he had been hurting and he was steeped in resentment, yet she knew he was a worthy person. And now she had agreed to go out with him again.

Anticipation overrode her caution, and she wondered what she would wear. A few more hours with Eli, she thought, eager and wary at the same time.

Eli's long-legged stride covered the ground easily, and he slid into his black sports car. She watched as he spun the car around and sped down the drive.

Feeling dazed, she touched her lips. He was a forceful man. A small inner voice corrected her—he was sexy and irresistible. She turned around to face her mother, who was gazing at her with a quizzical look.

Instantly Lara became aware of her disheveled appearance. Strands of hair had tumbled loose around her face. Her uniform was wrinkled and she guessed that her mouth was red from Eli's kisses. Her cheeks flamed from embarrassment.

"Who was that man?" Irena's blue eyes were filled with curiosity.

"Eli Ashton."

"One of the other Ashtons?" Irena persisted.

"Yes," Lara replied, heading back toward the dining room.

"Lara, do you know him?"

"Yes, I do," she answered, tucking stray strands back into her bun. "I'm going to dinner with him tonight."

"Criminy! My daughter and one of the Ashtons! Imagine that one!" Irena exclaimed loudly, clapping her hands together to Lara's horror.

"Mom! Shhh! It's a one-time deal. It's nothing."

"Nothing my foot! Is he taking you to dinner?"

"Yes, but after tonight I won't see him again," she said, trying to smooth her uniform. "I need to get back to the dining room to pick up the silver."

Her mother laughed with glee, heading for the kitchen, and

Lara suspected her mother would share this tidbit with the entire staff at the estate.

Lara returned to the dining room to pick up a sterling samovar and take it to the kitchen, where she met the gaze of her friend Franci. Her brown eyes were filled with curiosity, and Lara could guess why.

Franci had a jar of silver polish and a sponge and was shining one of the large sterling trays. Lara set the samovar down to start polishing it. The gleeful look in Franci's eyes confirmed her suspicions.

"When are you going to dinner with Eli Ashton?" Franci asked.

"How do you know that I'm having dinner with him?"

"Your mother told all of us," Franci replied, waving her hand, and although Franci and Lara were the only two in the kitchen, Lara knew that her mother had informed all the servants she could find.

"Mom's irrepressible."

"Your mom is exuberant She's so quiet around the Ashtons. I doubt if any of them have any idea how full of life she is. Even after all these years of working here."

"I'd just as soon she hadn't mentioned Eli Ashton to anyone. If word of this gets back to Lilah, you know there'll be trouble."

"Not too much to my way of thinking. You and your mom are too capable for Lilah to rock your boat very much. Besides, I don't think she'll care if Eli Ashton wants to take one of the maids to dinner. What are you wearing?"

"I have no idea," Lara replied.

"At lunch let me come help you pick out something."

"Franci, tonight isn't special. Eli isn't special," she said, but her words had a hollow ring. "I can't afford to have him in my life, and I know that he doesn't want to be in my life for any lasting period of time."

"You don't know that. I think he's interested in you."

"Temporarily, he is. I shouldn't have agreed to go out with him. He takes charge too much to suit me."

"You just don't like losing control."

"I guess I don't," Lara admitted. "He surely doesn't want to lose it, either."

"Sounds to me as if he rings your bell," Franci said smugly, and Lara frowned.

"No. He's arrogant and controlling and strong willed—"

"Ms. Kettle, are you calling the pot black?" Franci interrupted. "Admit it. You gave in because you like the guy and fireworks go off when you're around him."

"Sort of. He's tough and determined. I think his abrasiveness and control go back to Spencer's treatment of him and his family."

"We all knew Spencer and what a jerk he was," Franci declared, picking up the silver tray to carry it to the sink to wash off the polish. As water poured over the tray, Lara's thoughts were still on Eli.

Why hadn't she been able to stick with her refusal to go out with him? She suspected there wasn't a simple reason. On a sexual level she responded totally to him. This morning, she had seen yet another facet of Eli—his hurt and his rage toward Spencer. Deep down, a part of her wanted to save him from his rancor and disillusionment. "Yeah, right," she said aloud to herself. As if Eli Ashton needed saving from anything—or would let anyone else do so.

When she and Franci were ready to return the polished silver pieces to the dining room, Franci headed toward the door.

"It's time for our lunch break. Let's go up and pick out something for you to wear tonight. I want you to be a knockout."

"You don't even know him."

"I know he's what you need. Don't tell me you didn't enjoy being with him."

Lara inhaled, remembering the magical night with Eli. He carried her out of her drab routine into excitement that was difficult to resist. Giving a slight shake to her head, she clamped her lips together and pushed open the kitchen door, waiting for Franci to follow.

"I don't want a man intruding in my life. I've been there and done that, and I don't want to go through it again. Not now, anyway."

"Go out and enjoy yourself."

"Oh, Franci, you're a hopeless romantic! Let me introduce you to him."

"He would not react the same to me. From what you've told me, I think there's something special between the two of you."

"No, there's not. Like I said, you're a hopeless romantic."

"Well, whatever I am, let's put up this silver and go look in your closet. I want to help you pick out something." Franci persisted.

Lara thought about Eli on the way upstairs to her room. She thought about his kisses and how his fingers had lightly caressed her throat. She had returned his passion equally with her own, something she hadn't intended to do.

She needed to be firm with him tonight. Tonight might not be the last time he wanted to see her. As quickly as that thought came, she rejected it. She couldn't imagine a man like Eli Ashton pursuing her. Not beyond tonight. She'd hurt his pride by walking out on him the other night and now he probably wanted to do his own walking. Whatever his reasons, she was going to spend another evening with Eli Ashton—her pulse raced at the thought.

Excitement over finding Lara and anticipation of spending the evening with her drummed through Eli's body. But as he approached The Vines, the reading of the will replayed in his mind. With every mile the car covered, Eli's fury increased until he was in a blistering rage by the time he turned into the drive at The Vines and headed straight for the offices. Following a lifetime habit, his first inclination was to talk to his brother.

Eli slammed the car door and stormed through the tasting room where Jillian was talking to a group of tourists, explaining points about wine to them. He shot her a glance and she blinked, momentarily faltering but then catching herself and continuing.

Boiling inside, Eli strode to the stairs and took them two at time. In long steps he reached Cole's office and barged inside.

In a gray knit shirt, Cole sat behind his tidy desk, the one messy spot in a ruthlessly neat room. He took one look at Eli and shut off his computer.

"So what did the bastard do—cut us off without a cent?"

"No. He managed to make it a helluva lot more insulting than that." Unable to sit down, Eli paced the office. As he walked he yanked off his coat to fling it on a chair. Then he tore off his tie, balling it up and giving it a toss.

"So tell me already."

"He left one dollar to Mom and a dollar to each of us."

Cole's face tightened. "I shouldn't be surprised, but…hell." He looked away. His fingers thrummed once, twice, on the arm of the chair, then clenched into a fist. "When have we ever been able to count on him for anything? That's a rhetorical question," he added, shoving his chair back and standing. "Don't strain your brain trying to come up with an answer. So did he leave everything to Lilah?"

"No. His shares of Ashton-Lattimer Corporation went to Walker Ashton."

"Damn," Cole said as he rubbed the back of his head. "At the moment the stock isn't worth all that much. That stock's been shaky ever since the story broke about Spencer's first marriage and baby Jack."

"The stock will come back," Eli said, raking his fingers through his hair. "Twenty-thousand went to Charlotte Ashton."

"Considering the size of the estate, that's not much. Guess he didn't care for Charlotte."

"She probably has too much Sioux blood for him," Eli said, grinding out the words.

"And the rest of the estate?"

"The land, vineyards, winery, house and money were split between Lilah and the three children."

"His 'keeper' family. Well, I'm not surprised by that. I'm surprised by the rest."

"Walker's his golden-haired boy. When it was over, Walker told me I shouldn't have come, and Trace Ashton threatened to throw me out of the place."

"Did you hit anyone?" Cole asked, interested.

"I was on my best behavior. One more remark out of Trace, though, and I would have punched him. And I have to tell you, I was hoping he'd make one more remark."

Cole snorted. "I'm glad he didn't. This isn't the time to go punching people, with the cops looking for a murderer."

"I have an ironclad alibi, remember? I was working all night, and Randy from the bottling room was with me. Trace better leave me alone."

Cole shrugged. "He won't come looking for you, and you don't have any reason to go back to the estate."

"Lilah Ashton ran Mercedes and Jillian out of there, just like she tossed Anna and the baby out when they went to meet the family. Spencer and Lilah wouldn't have anything to do with Grant. Those damn people—" Eli spun around to place his hands on his hips and face his brother. "Cole, I'm calling our lawyer. We're going to try to break the will."

"Why?"

Eli glared at him. "What the hell do you mean, why? Do you want to let that son of a bitch get away with this?"

"I don't want or need a damned thing of his," Cole said, his voice low and intense. "We've done fine without him and his money. We can go right on doing fine. Go stick your hot head under some cold water. You aren't thinking straight."

"Like hell I'm not," Eli snapped. "It's not like the press will leave us alone if we don't sue. We're involved in Spencer's scandalous life no matter what we do. I let the rest of you talk me out of trying to get back Mom's heritage when we found out that Spencer committed bigamy. His marriage to Mom wasn't legal, so to my way of thinking, Spencer couldn't inherit all of grandfather's estate."

Cole's lips twisted. "You know what that makes us. Mom doesn't want to stir up more scandal."

"We can weather it. Now this damn will—we're going to contest it because we're Spencer's family. As much as I hate it, we have his blood in our veins."

Cole studied him out of narrowed eyes. "We'd better discuss

this as a family. If you go through with this, Mom, Dad, our sisters, all of us will be affected."

"Why don't we ask Grant and Anna and our in-laws over to talk things out, too?" Eli snapped with dripping sarcasm, clenching his fists and facing Cole, his irritation radiating toward his stubborn brother. "Or maybe you'd like to put it all on a spreadsheet first. Examine the bottom line."

"Considering outcomes is the adult way to deal with things," Cole said coldly. "I'm going to call them. Dixie, too. And Seth. They've got a stake in this."

"All right, dammit, ask them to be here." Eli raked his fingers through his hair again and let out his breath, knowing Cole with his practical way of thinking was probably right. "Let's get the family together to discuss it."

Cole looked at his watch. "Jillian is educating a group of tourists about wine. Mercedes is probably in her office, and Mom and Dad are at the house. I'll get them together, but give me some time to let Jillian finish what she's doing."

"Shannon can take over for her."

"I'll see," Cole said, picking up the phone. Eli strode to the window and tuned out his brother while in his mind's eye he saw the Ashton Estate vineyards. "Damn Spencer," he said under his breath.

Cole made two more calls and then turned to Eli. "All right, we're meeting at the house in the library thirty minutes from now. Jillian will be through then and the whole family will be present except Seth. That ought to suit you."

"You don't agree with me, do you?"

Cole rubbed his neck again. "I just want to give it thought before we fly off the handle and do something we'll regret down the road. I agree with Mom—we don't need this fight. We have a great life with Louret Vineyards now."

"We'd let Spencer trample us again. His damned will sets my blood boiling. I don't see what we have to lose."

"I can't see what we'd gain. I don't think we can break the will."

"That's for our lawyer and the courts to decide. And we can tie things up for a damn long time."

"You don't want to do that," Cole said. "Trace and Walker may have infuriated you, but they couldn't help what Spencer did any more than we could. And Paige and Megan Ashton—they haven't done a thing to hurt us."

"Oh, hell. Then I guess it boils down to my wrath toward Spencer. All right, I'll be in the library in thirty minutes."

"Bring a cooler head with you," Cole called after him as Eli swept up his coat and tie and left.

Thirty minutes later Eli's rage hadn't abated. He couldn't stand still so he paced the library, looking around at his family. Lucas, in jeans and a navy knit shirt, was sitting protectively beside Caroline on the sofa. Jillian and Mercedes sat with their heads together while Mercedes talked about a marketing strategy for Louret. Both sisters had light-brown hair—Mercedes's was curly and Jillian's wavy. Eli could see family resemblances in them, but he suspected it was only because he knew them so well.

Cole strode into the room and closed the door behind him. Dixie sat in a wing chair, and her eyes sparkled when her husband entered the room. Eli saw the look that passed between the two and for a moment forgot the will while envy stabbed him. Since his marriage, Cole seemed happier, more relaxed, a lot less the uptight, all-business brother he had been before Dixie had come into the family.

Eli liked both of his new in-laws, and he was glad for the happiness his brother and sister had found, but it was difficult to keep from being resentful because of his own disappointments.

"Sorry, I had a phone call, but I'm only—" Cole glanced at his watch "—four minutes late. Jillian, any chance Seth could get away and be here?"

Jillian looked up. "No. He'd like to, but he had an appointment he had to keep. He said to go on without him."

"We can wait until tonight," Cole offered, but she shook her head.

"No, there are enough of us to make a decision. Eli told us about the will," she said.

Eli faced his family. "You know what's in Spencer's will. What I want now is an agreement from the family to call Ridley Pollard and get him to look into contesting the will. And when we know what our legal options are, we can meet again to decide if we want to proceed or not. I still think we should have him look into whether or not Spencer could inherit from our grandfather when Spencer had committed bigamy. Sorry, Mom, but that's the truth."

"I know it is, Eli. I just want all of you to remember I had no knowledge of Spencer having a wife."

"We all know that, Mom," Eli said as the others added their reassurances. Jillian frowned at him, and he knew she didn't want their mom upset.

"First things first," Eli said. "If our lawyer says it's feasible to contest Spencer's will and that legally we have just cause, I want him to pursue the matter."

"I think we should hold off," Cole remarked, leaning forward and placing his elbows on his knees. "Mom doesn't want to fight the will. We all have a great life here at Louret. Besides, I don't think it will benefit us to contest the will. When Spencer made his will, he had a perfectly sound mind. He cut himself off from us years ago. Why should he have left us anything?"

"Because it was ours to begin with," Eli said. "And because he was our blood father."

"None of that meant a thing to him," Cole stated. "What do the rest of you think? Mom, let's hear from you."

Caroline glanced at Lucas and then looked at each of her children, her gaze returning to Eli. "I willingly gave up my father's inheritance years ago for my children. Thanks to all of you, Louret is successful beyond anything I could have imagined. Why stir up more anguish and turmoil? It would be a bitter, hateful battle and I would dread it," she said, worry clouding her hazel-green eyes.

"Dad?" Cole asked.

Lucas rubbed his jaw and was silent a moment as if he were still thinking about what to do. He turned his blue-eyed gaze on Eli. "I personally don't think you'll get anywhere if you do contest it," Lucas said. "I also think we all should give a lot of consideration to what your mother wants."

"Jillie," Cole said. "What do you think?"

"I don't think we should try to break the will. It'll just create more ill will between the families—"

"So who's going to care if it does?" Eli snapped.

"When Mercedes and I called on Paige and Megan, they were friendly. It was only Lilah Ashton who wasn't. I don't see any point continuing a feud that was Spencer's doing," Jillian argued.

"Dixie?" Cole asked his wife, and she shrugged.

"I'm too new to the family."

"You can have an opinion," Cole said. "This affects you as much as it will me."

"Sorry, Eli, but if it were left up to me, I'd leave it alone,"

Dixie said and Eli nodded. He liked Cole's wife and respected her opinion whether it agreed with his or not.

"I see Eli's side, but I see the other side, too," Mercedes said.

"I'm definitely in the minority," Eli admitted and raked his fingers through his hair.

"Eli, let's all think about it," Caroline suggested. "For another couple of weeks we'll consider talking to Ridley Pollard and the possibilities if we contest the will. We can get together again. That way there won't be a hasty decision to go ahead or to drop it.

"Can Cole at least ask Ridley whether we legally would stand any chance if we contest it?"

"Let's wait a couple of weeks," Cole replied before Caroline could answer.

Eli glared at his brother. "Spencer committed bigamy. Our grandfather's will referred to Spencer as 'my son-in-law' and Spencer was not our grandfather's son-in-law. This could mean we could legally contest the will and possibly revert Ashton Estate and Spencer's Ashton-Lattimer Corporation shares of stock back to Mom. You can't just walk away from all of Grandfather's holdings without giving it a lot of serious thought."

"We can if that's what makes Mom happy!" Cole snapped.

"Cole, Eli," Caroline said in a calm voice. "We'll think about it, but I don't want to pursue a course based on revenge," she said, looking at Eli, and he knew she was directing her remarks to him now.

He clamped his jaw closed and nodded. "All right," he said. "Just think about it."

"And that concludes our discussion," Lucas said, standing and offering his hand to Caroline. "Mom and I need to adjourn. We're having a party tomorrow night, and your mother says there's a lot to do to get ready."

"I want to get back to the office. I have a phone appointment in twenty minutes," Cole said, taking Dixie's hand while Eli merely nodded. He sat with his long legs stretched out in front of him, his arms crossed over his middle while he thought about the will.

As they left the room, Jillian caught up with Caroline. "I can help you get ready for the party," she said.

"I've got just the job for you," Caroline said, and their voices faded as they left the room and walked down the hall.

"Stop brooding over Spencer's will," Mercedes told Eli. "Besides, I have special news."

"What's that?" he asked, looking up at her.

"Our sales of Caroline Chardonnay set a record last month. On top of that, our 2000 Merlot won a silver medal from the *California Wine and Food* magazine."

"That's excellent, Mercedes! You should have announced that to everyone."

"I've seen the others and already told them. You were the last to hear."

Eli stood. "You're doing a great job."

"We're all doing a first-rate job," she said. "Our family is a mutual admiration society, but there's reason for it."

"Do me a favor. You think about this will and grandfather's will. Spencer stole all that from Mom. She's happy, but that land is rightfully hers."

"I'll think about it, but none of us want to make Mom unhappy. It's not worth doing that."

"I know," Eli said, raking his fingers through his hair. His thoughts jumped to Lara and this evening.

At the thought of seeing Lara again, his pulse began to beat faster. The memories of their only lusty night escalated his eagerness to be with her. He remembered the moment at the funeral reception when he had turned and looked into her light-brown eyes and sparks had jumped between them. Together they shared a volatile chemistry that sent his temperature rocketing just thinking about her.

Thank heaven he'd found her! This time he wanted to learn more about her. He wanted to take her to his bed, but he knew in order to spend more time with her, he needed to slow down.

During the afternoon Lara went through the chores of the day as if she were a robot. The only thing on her mind was Eli. When it was finally time to dress, she rushed to her room.

She bathed and pulled on a deep-purple, sleeveless cotton sheath that she and Franci had selected. With care, she pinned a silver rose on her dress. She wound her hair up on either side of her head and let the back fall freely. As she put pins in her hair, she remembered Eli taking them out slowly, sensually, building the mounting tension in her.

Just the sight of him today had turned her insides to jelly. But she reminded herself that she was only going to spend the evening with him—nothing more.

When she headed downstairs to get her car, Franci and her mother were waiting at the servants' entrance. "You look great. Knock him dead," Franci said.

"Well, that would make for an interesting evening," Lara remarked dryly. "Franci, I don't have any place in my life for Eli. Even if I did, I'd only be risking a broken heart."

"Lara, don't be so cautious," her mother urged. "The man is obviously interested in you."

"Sure, Mom. I'll see you two later."

She left and as she went to her car she said softly to herself,

"If I let myself be with this man, it would just be a matter of time until my heart would be in a million, tiny pieces."

She left to drive into Napa. It was a cool June evening, but she barely noticed the weather. All the way to town, her anticipation grew. She knew she shouldn't be seeing Eli and she shouldn't be looking forward to it so eagerly, but she did. "This is the last time we'll go out, Eli Ashton," she said softly, promising herself to guard her heart against the onslaught of his attention.

A fine lot of shielding her heart she had done this morning, finally yielding to his persistence about seeing her again.

When she parked in front of the restaurant, she watched him get out of his sports car and come forward to greet her. Just the sight of him made her pulse leap. To her surprise, he was in a charcoal sport coat, a pale-blue shirt that was open at the throat and gray slacks. She was thankful she had picked the deep-purple dress and her high-heeled purple sandals.

Eli Ashton—forceful, sexy, her undoing. She had heard Trace and Spencer talk about Louret wines. Now she could understand why Louret produced such premier wines. She had been the target of Eli's dogged determination. Applied to wine making his care and attention gently encouraged the winery's success. But with her, his attention was seductive and hot.

His gaze wandered languidly over her. Approval glowed in his emerald eyes as he reached out to take her hand. When his strong fingers closed around hers, she inhaled. How was she going to resist him when his slightest touch set her quivering?

"Come on. I have a surprise," Eli said. "You can leave your car here, and we'll come back to get it."

Curious she tilted her head. "You're not going to tell me ahead of time?"

He shook his head. "No. Let me surprise you," he said.

Six

He held the door open on the passenger side of his car, and Lara slid inside, buckling up and watching him as he walked around the car, remembering too clearly the first time she was with him.

He backed out and turned to leave the parking lot, driving to a nearby airfield to a waiting plane.

"I chartered a plane. We're flying to San Francisco for dinner and dancing."

"It sounds grand," she admitted. At the thought of dancing in his arms, she suddenly realized withstanding his appeal might just become even more difficult.

They entered the sleek white plane and were seated in comfortable window seats with a small table between them. A pretty blond, female attendant, dressed in gray slacks and a white blouse, moved around the cabin for a few minutes and then buckled up as soon as she had closed the door. When the plane taxied down the runway, Lara gazed out the window, but she was more aware of the man only a few feet from her.

As they took off, she inhaled, almost pressing her nose against the glass. "It's beautiful!" she exclaimed, glancing back at him to find him watching her with a faint smile.

"I'm glad you like it."

"I've never flown before," she admitted, once again aware of the chasm between his lifestyle and hers.

"Then that makes it all the better that I can do this with you for the first time. Especially if you like it."

As they circled over Napa and then headed south, she gazed out the window with fascination. "It's gorgeous! And we're going so fast!" Embarrassed, she turned back to him. "I sound like a child."

"Nothing wrong with that."

As soon as the plane had reached cruising altitude, the attendant brought them glasses of Chardonnay.

"Lara, this time while we're together, I'm going to learn something about you," Eli said.

"I lead the most ordinary life," she said, turning back to him. "I'm a maid at the Ashton Estate and I'm going to law school again in the fall. There you've got it."

He leaned forward, tracing his fingers along her cheek. "You look gorgeous tonight," he said. "Is this an antique pin?"

"Thank you," she replied, conscious of his light caress. "Yes. This one was my grandmother's."

"How did you get to the Ashton Estate? You said your mother is head housekeeper."

"She's been with them fifteen years, now, so I was eleven when she got the job with them. My father died from a heart attack the year before she went to work for the Ashtons."

"Sorry about your loss. Other than what Spencer put you through, do you like working there?"

"It's fine. The rest of the family are pleasant, and I have friends on the staff."

"I'm glad I went for the reading of the will or I never would have remet you. I didn't expect to ever be back at the estate— at least not for a long time."

"I'm here tonight, but only—" His fingers on her lips stopped her in midsentence.

"Wait," he commanded. "And no more of that nonsense that we can't see each other because you're a maid and I'm a wine-maker. Or that I'm my father's son."

"You're forceful, Eli. You go after what you want. I told you that the first night we were together."

"I've had to be forceful. Spencer walked out on us when I was eight years old. The night he left, I overheard him tell my mother that he didn't want any part of us. He agreed to child support, but that's the only way he's ever acknowledged our existence. He called us brats."

"How dreadful!"

"That was Spencer," Eli said with a shrug. "When he came out of the library, I tried to hit him for leaving us, and he slapped me hard," Eli said, resentment creeping into his voice.

Lara's heart clenched and she reached out to squeeze his hand. When her fingers closed around his, Eli's dark eyebrows arched. "That was a long time ago and the hurt has diminished with the years. He left us with the vineyard that had belonged to my grandmother. My mother was alone with four little children and she didn't know how she was going to deal with any of it, but she did."

"What a frightening time for all of you!"

"Thank heavens for Dad—Lucas. To me he's Dad. He started teaching Mom the winery business. He gave me jobs, just simple things when I was eight, but I was tall for my age and before long, I got some muscles."

In spite of knowing that she shouldn't be finding reasons to like him, Lara couldn't help seeing the honorable side to Eli, who had done all he could for his family and helped build Louret Vineyards into a fine boutique winery. "I've heard Trace and Spencer talk about Louret on occasion—a few times I even heard Walker talking about it to them. It infuriated Spencer that the Louret Vineyards had better wine than Ashton Estate."

"I'm glad," Eli said harshly, gazing past her. "Maybe that's why I go after what I want. I've had to for so long, and it's gotten to be a habit. At first it was sheer survival—trying to help my mother any way I could. But later, when I was older, with Dad and my younger brother, Cole, our wine beat Spencer's. He never acknowledged our accomplishments."

"He was envious and seething. I know he was determined to develop better wines."

"So I heard. I know he hired Alexandre Dupree who is a noted winemaker. A premier winery takes a lot of work and attention to small details. Our whole family is involved in our business. My sister Mercedes has increased sales with her marketing. My baby sister, Jillian, has been a super worker. She's studied viticulture and enology at U.C. Davis. Just recently she revamped our tasting room, which has been her big project. When I was a kid, I wanted to make everything right for my mother. I guess I still do," he said, and a faraway look filled his eyes until Lara wondered if he had even forgotten her presence.

She held his hand and knew that beneath his capability and his sophistication, he still hurt, and she saw how wrong she had been to lump him with Spencer. Although far too bossy and harsh, Eli was an admirable person.

His attention returned to her and his anger vanished. "If it means anything to you, I've never told anyone outside the family that before. Our family is pretty close-knit. We have tiffs, but they're superficial. We've had to pull together for too many years."

"That's wonderful, Eli."

"Do you have any brothers or sisters?"

"No. I'm the only one so I feel a responsibility for my mother."

"She's got a good job and an elegant place to live. Is her health all right?"

"Yes. For years she's had to do Spencer and Lilah Ashton's bidding. She's earned a rest and time to do what she likes. I want to get her out of there. That's my goal and the reason why this isn't such a great idea tonight. I don't want to get entangled."

He leaned closer until he was inches away while he slid his fingers over her collar. "I wouldn't want to divert you from your goals. I just want to enjoy some time with you."

She smiled at him. "That's comforting to know."

The attendant appeared again with a snack tray, and Lara declined. Eli shook his head and declined having any also. Why did she always lose her appetite when she was with him? Lara wondered. Why couldn't she see Eli as an ordinary man?

"Penny for your thoughts," he said. Distracting her, he ran his fingers down her bare arm and then moved his hand to her knee. She inhaled and met his gaze.

He looked at her with an intensity that made her feel desirable and pretty. It also made her tingle. Her nipples tightened, pushing against her lacy bra and purple dress. Heat coiled low in her while memories of Eli's strong, naked body tormented her. Silently she once again vowed to avoid repeating their night of lust. She intended to resist him and hold fast to her resolution to shun complications. Especially six-foot, sexy complications.

"I was wondering about your daily life. Tell me about your winery," she said.

"You'll have to come see it. It's not big, but I think it's attractive. Jillian has done a bang-up job renovating the tasting room. We've had a lot of tourists for this early in summer."

"I think everyone is getting a large number of tourists," Lara said. "I've heard Trace and Paige talking about the numbers."

A few minutes later the attendant returned to take their glasses while the pilot announced that they were beginning their descent into San Francisco. The sun was setting in the west, but Lara could see the Bay.

"It's beautiful!" she gasped, wondering how many flights she would have to take to become as blasé about flying as Eli.

She watched until they touched down and sat back, smiling at him. "That was incredible!"

"You're easy to please, but then, the first flight is usually memorable and fascinating."

"How old were you when you had your first flight?"

He shook his head. "Probably about seven when some of us flew to Chicago. Spencer was giving a speech to a group of bankers on the future of investment banking and Cole and I got to go along, but the girls were too young and had to stay home."

"Do you remember the flight?"

"Not particularly. I remember wrestling with Cole until we both were in trouble. Here we are," he announced as the plane taxied to a stop.

They left the plane and hurried to a waiting black limo that whisked them downtown to one of the tallest buildings in the city. They took an elevator to a restaurant on the top floor. They followed the maître d' through an elegant room decorated with a thick red carpet, paneled walls and muted lighting. Across the room from their window table a piano player sang and couples were already dancing.

The white linen cloth held a flickering candle and a vase of deep red roses, and the window offered them a panoramic view of the city. It was dusk and lights were winking.

With Eli life was enchanting and seductive. As he discussed the wine with the waiter, she enjoyed watching Eli. His brown hair was short, combed in place. Candlelight highlighted his prominent cheekbones, throwing the planes of his cheeks in shadow. There was a craggy, rugged look to him that his personality matched, yet he was appealing and sexy.

They ordered wine and steaks, but just like their last dinner together, there was too much to talk about, and their wine and the juicy steaks were barely touched.

"Who do you think Spencer's murderer is?" she asked, and Eli shrugged.

"Who knows? I imagine there are a lot of people who hated him."

"The authorities questioned everyone at the estate. I suppose they questioned all of your family."

He nodded. "Briefly two detectives were out. I was working almost all night the night Spencer was shot and I have another worker with me so I had an alibi, if you're wondering and are too polite to ask."

"No!" She felt her cheeks flush and was sorry she had brought up the subject. "I don't think you killed him. You're not a murderer."

"You sound so sure," he said, giving her a quizzical look.

"I think you're a fine person, Eli," she said, taking his hand. The moment she touched him, she saw a flicker in his eyes and she knew she was taunting a tiger again. He turned his hand to hold hers. "I imagine all your efforts are directed at Louret Vineyards," she said, trying to get back on a less personal note.

"That's the truth," he said, while his thumb ran back and forth across her knuckles. "I hope we have a predictable summer this year. Two years ago we had a great crop in spite of the roller-coaster summer weather, cool and wet and then hot and dry. In spite of it, I think we'll have a terrific Cabernet that year. We had a superb one in 2000. It's been aged in American and French oak for almost two years. We've got a Chardonnay that's been aged on the yeast for six years and it's going to be great."

"In spite of living at the Estate, I don't know anything about the vineyards or wine."

"The vineyard is my life. My whole family's actually. I think in the future, we're going to have to get more into blended wines. It looks like they'll be the fad." Candlelight was reflected in his green eyes and he gave her a heated look as he continued to stroke her knuckles.

"Is that okay or something bad? You don't sound happy," she said, aware of the touch of his thumb. Her gaze lowered to his mouth. She drew a deep breath and tried to pay attention to what he was telling her when what she really wanted was to kiss him again.

"It's new and I'm not as fond of blends. Jillian has a great background, and we can let her take charge of blends now that she has the tasting room finished." He raised Lara's hand to his lips to brush a kiss on her knuckles. "I want you to see our winery."

"Maybe," she said cautiously. He smiled at her, a knowing, satisfied smile as if he were certain she would capitulate and do what he wanted.

"Enough about Louret Vineyards. How many hours will you take in law school in the fall?" he asked.

"Twelve probably," she answered, "since I'll continue to work."

"What kind of law are you interested in? Any specialty?"

"I like research. I don't intend to be a trial lawyer and I'm not interested in criminal law. I find it depressing to go to the courthouse. Oil and gas law interests me."

"Why is that?"

"I figure it'll be easier to get a job with a large company. There should be plenty of business in California, and I'd like to live in a large city."

"Good reasons. Too bad you don't have your degree in dealing with wills," he remarked dryly.

All the time they talked, he played with her hand or he reached out to caress her nape. Every stroke fueled her desire, but she was still determined to avoid getting too carried away. Finally he stood and offered his hand. "Let's dance."

Lara walked with him to the dance floor that was inside the dimly lit restaurant. When she stepped into Eli's embrace, she could feel his warmth, smell his aftershave. As they moved together, he pulled her closer.

"This is what I wanted. Better than the steak. You said your goal was to get your mother out of the Ashton job. How do you plan to do that?"

Lara looked up at him. "When I get established as a lawyer, I intend to move her in with me, maybe not into my house if she doesn't want to, but somewhere nearby. She deserves that and she's taken care of me my whole life. Now I want to take care of her."

"That's an excellent goal."

"That's why I don't want anything to interfere with school and getting my degree. Or passing the bar exam," Lara said, her thighs brushing Eli's. Too clearly, she remembered being held in his arms while they both were naked, remembered his warm breath on her ear as it was now. "There's no place for a man or a relationship in my life right now. I'm twenty-six. There will be time later."

"Baby," he teased. "I'm thirty-seven."

"Senior citizen," she flung back. "Or maybe you're heading for a midlife crisis. Thirty-seven and you've never been married?"

"Nope. I've had some disastrous relationships that I'd just as soon forget. Twenty-six and you've never been married?"

"No. I've had some disastrous relationships of my own that I'd just as soon forget. Some domineering men that I've known."

"So to add to my sins, I'm lumped in with the domineering men from your past?"

She looked away from his piercing gaze. "Maybe you are. You do fall in the masterful class."

"Hopefully I can make up for that in some manner with you," he answered solemnly.

"It's back to law school for me. That's why I don't want to get involved with anyone at the moment. I can deal with a man later."

"Did you ever think you could do both?"

"No. Law school is demanding, and I want to maintain my grades."

"You know that old saying about 'All work and no play makes Jane a dull girl—"

"Well, that's Jane's problem. I have an agenda and I intend to stick to it. Actually, I would guess you're focused when you want to be."

"I suppose. I'm thankful I met you in the summer when law school is out." He leaned down to trace her ear with his tongue and she closed her eyes. It was heaven on earth to dance in his arms and be held close, to move in unison with him. For a time tonight, she might as well enjoy herself. The witching hour would come soon enough when she'd have to return to her world and tell Eli goodbye.

She realized there was a lot more to him than she first thought. He wasn't a playboy and he wasn't like Spencer. Spencer thought only of himself. Eli put his family first in his life and she had to admire him for that. When he told her about his life, though, he sounded disillusioned and he was a fine man, too kind to go through life as dissatisfied as he sounded.

The next dance was a fast number, and Eli was adept and sexy as he moved, spinning her around and then pulling her back into his arms. One time he stopped, took her hand and hurried back to their table to shed his coat and then they returned to the dance floor. Too well she remembered his bare, muscled chest. As they danced his eyes were hooded, hot with desire.

Fast and slow, they went from one dance to another and sat down only when the piano player took a break. As soon as the pianist returned they were back on the dance floor.

"You like to dance, don't you?" she remarked.

"What I like is touching you, holding you and looking at you," he said in a husky, sensual tone that quickened her pulse. "Dancing allows me to do that.

"I want you, Lara," he whispered in her ear, turning her insides to jelly.

"Stop trying to seduce me," she said, leaning back and putting a degree of distance between them.

"I merely answered your question. And when you move—that's seduction!"

"It's getting hot here on the dance floor."

"I can think of some remedies. Come here," he said, taking her hand. They walked off the dance floor and out of the dining room to the elevators. She looked at him quizzically while her pulse drummed. She was not going to another hotel room with him.

"What are we doing, Eli?"

"You said you were hot. There's a terrace on the roof and it'll be cool."

When the elevator opened, they stepped inside. He pushed the button and then turned to put one hand on the wall beside her while he leaned close. "I know I'm on fire," he said in a husky voice. He was too close, his mouth too tempting and memories too vivid.

She put her hand against his chest, "Eli—"

"At last," he whispered and leaned down to cover her mouth with his. Her heart thudded as his lips pressed hers and his tongue touched hers. She opened her lips to him, melting when his arms closed around her. She slid her arms around his neck while her drumming heartbeat drowned out all other noises. She was only aware of Eli's strong body against hers, his mouth on hers, fiery and magic all at once.

She slid her hands over his chest and desire swept her with the force of a forest fire. She was hot, aching for him, holding him and stroking his back, all her resolutions about resistance going up in smoke.

He wound his fingers in her hair, tumbling her locks and

spilling her pins. A cold draft of air hit her and she pushed against his chest. She twisted and saw the elevator doors were open. "Eli!"

He raised his head, and the blatant need in his eyes heightened her own desire.

"The doors—" she whispered, stunned by the consuming look he was giving her.

"Eli—" she said again.

He pushed a button and the doors closed and they started down. When he reached for her, she went into his arms, wanting him with all the pent-up need that he had built within her all evening.

The doors opened to the restaurant and two laughing couples entered the elevator. Lara blushed as she stepped out. They gathered their things and then left.

When they were in the limo, he pulled her into his arms to kiss her again.

But knowing they weren't alone, she quickly cut him off. He made her lose all restraint. He brought out the dangerous, impulsive side of her. She had so much to lose—but she couldn't deny she wanted him, too. At the airport they boarded the plane. As they taxied to the end of the runway, many of the interior lights switched off. Eli pulled her onto his lap and wrapped his arms around her waist after buckling them both into the seat.

"Now if you want to see a pretty sight, look at San Francisco when we take off."

She wound her arm around his neck while she turned her attention to the window. In minutes they had clearance and the plane gained speed, finally lifting into the air and climbing.

She looked at the sparkling array of lights below, far more than she had seen from the tall building. "It's beautiful!" she gasped. She turned to look at him. "I sound like a country bumpkin, don't I? But it is dazzling! Thank you for this—for the whole evening."

"I'm glad you're enjoying yourself. You have a passion for life, Lara."

"I have a passion for you," she said in a soft, sultry voice. Inhaling, he tightened his arms and kissed her, taking up where they'd left off in the elevator.

When he reached for the zipper of her dress, she caught his hands. "We're not alone."

"The flight attendant is gone. She stayed over in San Francisco. The pilot is busy and I'm just kissing and touching you a little and you like it, don't you?"

"Far too well," she whispered before his mouth covered hers again. His hands played over her breasts and she ached to get rid of the barriers of clothes, but knew she needed to guard her heart against the onslaught of this charismatic, strong-willed man.

They flew back to Napa and Eli drove her to the restaurant where he parked near her car. He cut the engine and turned to her. "My family is having a party to welcome some new neighbors tomorrow night. A couple has started a vineyard north of us and my mother wants to get to know them and introduce them to the neighborhood.

"That's friendly, Eli, even if they are competition. Although Louret Vineyards doesn't have to worry about competition from a new vineyard."

"No. They really are new at this and they're doing it on a shoestring, which also gets my mom's sympathy."

"Your mother sounds like a great person."

"She's a blue-ribbon mom," he said, and Lara could hear

the warmth in his voice when he talked about his mother. "Right now, residing with us, we have both my half brother, Grant Ashton, and Jack, Spencer's illegitimate baby, and Jack's aunt Anna. Grant's niece, Abigail, was with us. My mother would take in just about anyone if she thought he needed a place." Eli drew circles on Lara's knee with his forefinger while he talked. His casual touch was fiery. She hoped she didn't indicate the depth of the reaction she was having to his slight touch. "I want you to go the party with me, Lara. It's casual. No big deal."

Startled she stared at him. "I can't meet your family—"

"It's informal," he repeated. "C'mon. It'll be a far more interesting party if you're there, and of course you can meet my family. Half of Napa already knows them."

"Eli, we shouldn't get so involved with each other," she said. Her arguments seemed to run off him like water off glass.

"Lara, I know you're going to law school in the fall. But we can be friends and go out together this summer. The party is at seven. I'll pick you up at half past six."

"Are you listening to me?" she asked.

"I want you with me and it'll just be a bunch of people from this area. My family will be friendly."

"I'm not worried about your family being unfriendly."

"Good. I'll be there to pick you up." He leaned close to kiss the corner of her mouth, touching her lips with his tongue. Before she could turn her head to kiss him, he leaned away. "I promise you'll like my family."

"Do you understand the word *no?*"

"All too well. I don't want to hear it now."

She closed her eyes and gave up. As his arms wrapped around her, he kissed her soundly. One more night out with him. A family gathering with neighbors. Where could the harm be in that, and how risky would a few hours with his family be to her heart?

She pushed against his chest, determined to keep his hot kisses from escalating. "All right, Eli. Tomorrow night for the family party. I'll drive to your house."

"Nope. We did that tonight. I want to pick you up."

She sighed in exasperation. "You'll have to come around to the servants' entrance. I'll see to it that someone will let you in the gate."

"That works for me. I'm not overly welcome at the Ashton Estate anyway. Having you at the party will make it a whole lot better."

"I need to get names straight. Your brother is Cole."

"And he has a new wife, Dixie."

"Mercedes and Jillian are your sisters."

"Right. Jillian is married now to Seth Benedict. Seth has a little girl, Rachel. They're all friendly people," he repeated.

"I'm not worried about them," she said, leaning closer to him and pronouncing her words slowly as if he were deaf or couldn't get through his head what was bothering her.

"There's no need to worry about 'us' because there is no 'us,'" he said.

"You say that, but then you turn right around and ask me out again. There will be an 'us' if we keep seeing each other."

"No, we'll agree to keep this casual. In the fall you'll go back to college and I'll be working night and day at harvest."

"Eli, to put it bluntly, you're a complication I don't need in my life now."

"You're pragmatic, practical. You have solid, admirable goals for your future. I think you'll stick to them whether we spend time together or not."

"You can't always predict whether you will or won't fall in love."

"Neither of us has time for love," he said. "We both control our lives, and we're not going to let someone else step in and interfere."

"Maybe that's why we clash even though there's an attraction—we're constantly fighting for control."

He arched one dark eyebrow and nodded. "I suppose. The attraction is bigger than the clash."

"Do you think so?" she asked sweetly, and he narrowed his eyes.

"See what you think," he growled, and pulled her to him to kiss her passionately. His kiss possessed her, made her his woman, spoke volumes about wanting her that he never put into words. His tongue stroked her mouth sensually, stunning her because she had never felt this way before.

With her heart drumming, she wound her arms around his neck and returned his kiss, trying to have as devastating an effect on him as he did on her. Her toes curled and heat scorched her. Desire was compelling, making her want him just as she had that first night, but she fought her feelings and pushed away.

"I need to go," she said, and climbed out of his car. He got out and walked around. He pulled her close beside him as they strolled to her car. She turned to him. "It was a wonderful, magical night that I will never forget. When I'm with you, I'm Cinderella."

"I hardly qualify for Prince Charming," he said. "I can't go that route."

She didn't tell him that he did qualify for Prince Charming in too many ways.

"And as for Cinderella," he continued, "She never gave Prince

Charming this much trouble. She was never as feisty as you. She was dazzled and simply fell at his feet."

"Don't hold your breath on that one," Lara remarked dryly, and he wrapped his arms around her and leaned down to continue where he had left off with his kisses, creating a storm of need in her.

She trembled as she kissed him. She wanted him with all her being, wanted another night of wild passion.

Her arms went beneath his coat, and she ran her hands over his back, remembering every muscular inch of him, mentally envisioning him naked and loving her. She was on dangerous ground and she knew it. With all the willpower she could muster, she broke off their kiss and leaned away. "I have to go now. It was a fabulous evening."

"Yes," he said in a husky voice. "Until tomorrow night." He opened her car door and closed it behind her, waved and then strode away to his car.

She started her engine and backed out, heading toward the highway. He followed her, staying close until she turned into the Ashton Estate. Then he turned around and drove north to his home.

She sighed and shook her head. She was on fire with wanting him. Eli was bitter and sounded jaded about love, as if he had given up on it. Yet she could see the heart of gold that he hid.

She thought back to the spectacular night they'd had and the exciting man that Eli was. She was charmed by the references to Cinderella. Even though Eli denied it—and he was far more lordly and earthy than Prince Charming—he was a prince to her. For five more minutes, she decided, she would believe in the fairy tale and then she would return to her practical world where fairy tales didn't happen.

She went to her tiny room in the servants' quarters and slipped into a nightgown. She ached with frustration and unrequited desire.

Tomorrow night she would meet his family. Trepidation filled her. He swore he wouldn't get serious, yet why was he taking her home to a family party? And what on earth would she wear!

The following night she took a deep breath and went downstairs and outside to wait at the servants' entrance. The back door opened and Irena and Franci stepped outside.

"Mom!" Lara smiled at her mother and friend. "I take it you both want to meet Eli."

"Yes and since you're standing out here, I guessed that you weren't planning on bringing him inside where we can meet him."

"No, I'm not. I prevailed on one of the gatekeepers to let him in, but Eli isn't welcome here. At least not with Trace, Lilah or even Walker." She heard a car and turned to see Eli circling the house. "Here he comes." Right on time, she watched as he drove up and climbed out of the car, coming to meet her.

Convinced that Lilah Ashton would be furious to find one of her staff associating with Eli, Lara had intended to get right into his car the minute he arrived. She was anxious to get into the haven of the car and drive away from Ashton Estate. Then she forgot all about Lilah Ashton as Eli stepped out of his car and came toward her. He wore chinos, a tan knit shirt and brown loafers and her mouth went dry.

Fighting the urge, she smiled at him. Solemnly he let his gaze drift over her and then met her gaze.

"You look gorgeous," he said in a husky voice and she was aware of her silky blouse and black slacks, her high-heeled sandals. He glanced beyond her. "Is this your mother?" he asked, walking up and offering his hand to Irena.

"Mom, Franci. This is Eli Ashton. Eli, I'd like you to meet my mother, Irena Hunter and my friend Franci."

"I've heard about you and now I'm glad to meet you," Franci said, shaking hands with Eli.

"Yes, Lara talks about you all the time," Irena said.

"Mom! I do no such thing!"

Irena, Franci and Eli all laughed. Irena's eyes sparkled with delight. "You two have a fine evening."

"We will, Mrs. Hunter. It was nice to meet you both." Eli linked Lara's arm in his and they walked to his car.

"Your mother is good-natured."

"She enjoys herself and everyone around her."

He took Lara's hand. Her back prickled with sudden apprehension. She wanted to get Eli off the estate as fast as possible. She would never understand why he'd insisted on picking her up. If any of the Ashtons saw her with Eli, she was as good as fired. At the car, when Eli opened the door on the passenger side, she glanced back at the house. Her heart leaped to her throat at what she saw behind them.

Seven

A woman walked along the drive. Lara's heart missed a beat. Then, to her relief, she recognized Charlotte, who waved and smiled. Lara returned the wave, and Eli followed her gaze. "That's Charlotte Ashton, isn't it?"

"Yes," Lara answered when she slid into his car. She watched Eli go around the car. As he did, he waved to Charlotte, and as soon as he started driving, Lara turned to him.

"You don't know Charlotte, do you?" Lara said.

"No, I don't, but I'd like to. I don't think she was close with Spencer, and he only gave her a token bequest in his will."

"Charlotte is friendly and has always been kind to me. Actually, I feel rather close to her. She doesn't treat me like a servant. Sometimes I feel like woodwork to some of them, mainly Lilah. I don't think they even see me, but not Megan or Charlotte. Both of them seem like friends."

Eli glanced at Lara. He wished he could take care of her, but he knew with her independent nature, she would have none of it. He wanted to sweep her off her feet, but it was obvious from all her arguments about going out with him that he had to back off or else he would lose her.

Last night he had wanted to get a hotel room and take her there, to make passionate love to her again, but she would have been gone like a flash if he had made any such overtures. He'd overcome her arguments so far about spending time together, but he was treading as lightly as if he were in a minefield. He didn't expect this relationship to end any less disastrously than others had for him. Yet Lara was different from all other women he had known—more exciting, more independent, sexier.

Lara was quiet when he drove under the iron arch of curving vines that protected the entrance to Louret Winery and swept up to the house. "Here we are," he said.

"Your home is beautiful."

"That's my mom's doing," he explained proudly. "It's comfortable, a real plus in my book. I'll show you my suite when we get a chance."

"I'm surprised you live at home."

"I often work until three or four in the morning, so it's handy to fall in bed here."

"I don't think you trust a lot of people," she said, "but you trust your family."

Annoyed, he shot her a stormy glance and then shrugged. "I suppose that describes my life. I hadn't ever thought about it. People have a way of disappointing me, but my family doesn't." He drove around to the back where people were congregated.

"That's sort of bleak, Eli."

"So, do I have your sympathy?" he asked softly, cutting the motor and leaning close to her.

"You don't need sympathy or want it," she said, drawing herself up. "You're strong and self-sufficient and—"

"Don't tell me arrogant again," he said. For a moment he thought he might have elicited her sympathy, but it had vanished with his question. There was fire in her eyes and she had put that wall up that kept her heart shielded. He knew he had his own protective barriers, too.

"Come meet everyone," he said, climbing out of the car and walking around to hold her door. He took her hand, but, to his amusement, she shook free of him. "I may be arrogant, but you're as independent as a person can be," he said.

Even though she smiled sweetly, he knew that demure countenance hid a will of iron. He wondered if there was a time she would ever let someone take care of her even in little ways.

A small combo played: a bass, a fiddle, a clarinet and a drum. Brisket was being smoked in a cooker by the caterers and tempting smells wafted in the air. Round tables, each with a yellow tablecloth, were scattered across the patio. Centered on the tables were pots of pink geraniums with clusters of balloons anchored to the pots.

"How pretty this is, Eli!" Lara exclaimed.

"My mother has a knack for decorating. There's an artistic streak in the family. It bypassed me, but my mother and my sister Jillian have it. Come meet all of them."

While uniformed caterers served drinks, Eli took Lara's arm to lead her through the crowd toward an attractive woman in a lavender blouse and gray slacks.

"Mom," he said, and the woman with dark-blond hair that was stylishly short, turned to smile at him. When she looked at Lara and extended her hand, her hazel-green eyes were friendly. "This is Lara Hunter," Eli said. "Lara, meet my mom, Caroline Sheppard."

Lara smiled as she shook hands briefly with his mother.

"Welcome to The Vines. I'm glad you could join us tonight." Caroline turned to catch the arm of a slender, gray-haired man. Twinkling blue eyes met Lara's gaze as he held out his hand.

"Lara, this is my dad, Lucas Sheppard," Eli said. Lucas enveloped Lara's hand in a warm handshake that made her feel welcome.

"You'll have to get Eli to give you a tour," Lucas said. "Just don't let him talk about grapes all night."

"Maybe I'll learn something about vineyards," Lara replied pleasantly, aware of Caroline's curious gaze still on her.

"I'm going to introduce her around," Eli said, taking her arm to steer her to another group of people.

Lara met a dizzying array of friends and relatives and tried to get his immediate family members firmly fixed in her mind.

When he introduced her to the new neighbors for whom the party was being held, she was surprised at how young they both looked.

"Lara, this is Kent and Rita Farrar," Eli said. "They have Farrar Vineyards just to the northwest of us."

Lara shook hands with a tall, blond man and a slender blond woman dressed in a denim skirt and white cotton blouse.

"This is so nice of you and your family to welcome us to the area like this," Kent Farrar said.

"Glad to have you as neighbors."

"If we can get half as tasty wine as Louret Vineyards, we'll be thrilled," Rita Farrar added with a smile.

"We've worked at developing these wines for a long time now," Eli replied. "It takes time and weather and luck."

"And ability," Kent Farrar said. He held up his glass. "This Cabernet Sauvignon is delicious."

"It's a 2001 release. An excellent year," Eli answered. They discussed wine briefly and then Eli took Lara's arm to introduce her to other guests.

"The Farrars look young to be starting a vineyard," Lara said as they walked away from the couple.

"Kent told me they got out of college last year. His grandfather put up the money for their winery."

"I'd think they'd want experience working for someone else for a few years first. I hope they succeed," she said.

"We've had some economically hard times. That's why the Farrars got their acres at a bargain price. Competition is getting fierce, too."

"Your family is nice to welcome them. After all, they'll be your competition."

He shrugged. "That's my mom and dad—Mr. And Mrs. Friendly. We're established and we've weathered the downturns. We can afford to be friendly."

"I'm glad," she said, squeezing Eli's arm. The moment she touched him, Eli looked down at her and covered her hand. A look passed between them and for a moment the world disappeared. Only Eli existed and she wanted him with all the hunger she had felt that first night when they had abandoned logic for passion.

A newly arrived guest called a greeting to Eli and shattered the moment. Eli's fingers tightened slightly on her arm. "Come meet my brother Cole and his wife, Dixie. He's Mr. Dollars-and-Cents. He does an excellent job on the business end of things even if he is a bit stubborn and doesn't always understand some of the expenses I have."

"I suspect your brother thinks you're a bit stubborn, too," she said with amusement. "You're fortunate to have such a wonderful, big family," she said.

Before they could reach Cole and Dixie, a man came up to Eli and shook his hand. He had broad shoulders, fine lines in his face and looked to be in his early forties. His green eyes hinted that he might have Ashton blood in him, but she knew it wasn't Eli's brother. The man smiled broadly and Eli flashed a rare smile in return. "Lara, this is Grant Ashton, my half brother from Nebraska. Grant, this is my friend, Lara Hunter."

Grant's large hand enfolded Lara's as he shook her hand and smiled at her. There was an earthiness and strength to both men that had been evident the moment she first met them.

"I'm glad to meet you," she said.

"Glad to meet you. Are you getting introduced to too many Ashtons?"

She laughed. "No. I'm delighted to meet them, and everyone has made me feel welcome."

"This family excels at that. They've made me feel welcome, too." Grant turned to Eli. "The Farrars are overjoyed with this party. They're like two friendly pups."

"It's Mom and Dad's deal. The Farrars can direct their thanks to them."

"I haven't had a chance to talk to you, but I heard about what happened yesterday at the reading of the will. Spencer stayed a bastard to the very end."

"I should've known not to expect anything," Eli said grimly.

"I can't believe that you did. He tossed people out of his life like unwanted trash." Grant shook his head. "But this isn't a night to discuss Spencer. I don't want to think about him. I'd better give my regards to Lucas and Caroline. I just got here and haven't talked to them yet. It was great to meet you, Lara." Grant walked away, and Eli took Lara's arm again.

"Grant didn't even know Spencer was his father until this past year. He saw a picture of Spencer on TV and recognized him from a picture his mother had."

"What a shock!" Lara exclaimed, looking over her shoulder at Grant. "I've heard talk floating around the estate about the news. And, of course, the press picked up the lurid details and scandalous rumors."

"They weren't just rumors. It was the truth. One more scandal that Spencer brought down on everyone he ever touched. Grant is Spencer's first son. Spencer walked out on his family in Nebraska more than forty years ago. Grant is a salt-of-the-earth man," Eli continued to explain.

"I don't know how Spencer had such fine sons when he was so selfish," she remarked.

"Other people have raised us, not Spencer," Eli replied, and bitterness laced his voice.

Lara wrapped her arm more tightly in his. "Let go of your bitterness, Eli. Spencer is gone forever."

"His legacies and scandals and hurtful actions aren't," Eli ground out the words. Taking a deep breath, he tried to shake off the bad feelings. He smiled at her. "Come see our vines." Eli led her away from the party, and she saw row upon row of vines ahead of her. When they got close, she saw that the vines already bore clusters of tiny green grapes.

"There are lots of grapes."

"We'll thin the clusters. Then when they ripen, I walk, sample and taste the grapes in every vineyard block daily. That's the only way to tell when the grapes reach the necessary sugar levels. Then we'll know it's time to harvest."

"Is that difficult?"

"Just busy. In harvest, we work around the clock. We use the cordon method for the vines," he said, pointing to the wire trellises stretched along each row that supported the vines. "With this method, pruning and tying the vines are simple." Eli snapped off a sucker he spotted and brushed his fingers over the tiny grapes. "These are Pinot Noir grapes, a thin-skinned grape and one of the oldest varieties. Are you familiar with the grapes at the estate?"

"No, not really."

"I know they grow Pinot Noir." Eli knelt to pull a weed away from the vine, and he picked up a handful of dirt. "This is the lifeblood of Louret—this soil, the vines and the grapes," he said solemnly.

"You like your job, don't you?"

"I can't imagine doing anything else." He stood and brushed off his hand as his gaze roamed over the acres. "Sixty-five acres to produce some excellent wines. We have our Cab, Pinot Noir, Merlot and Petite Verdot grapes. We buy Chardonnay grapes. Beyond these rows are the Cab grapes next. As far as the wine is concerned, my taste runs to our Merlot. I don't know your favorite. What is it?"

"I don't know wines like you do, but I mostly prefer Cabernet Sauvignon."

"Great. That's what we're serving tonight. That and our Caroline Chardonnay." He looked around. "When I have a problem or my temper boils over, I come out here and work."

She gazed up at him. It was obvious Eli had inherited Spencer's hot temper, yet she knew he could hold that temper in check—as he had done after the reading of the will.

He took her hand. "Come with me and I'll show you our horses and the lake. Over there," he said, pointing east, "we have a carriage house and a guest cottage. Right now, Grant is living in the carriage house, and Anna and Jack are in the guest cottage." Eli took Lara's hand. "First of all, let me show you our tasting room. I told you that Jillie did it over this spring. She did a great job."

They walked toward a building set amid the vineyards to the west. Like Eli's family home, the winery was an inviting structure. It was two stories with peaked roofs and a large front porch.

After they crossed the porch and stepped inside, Eli switched on lights to reveal exposed ceiling beams. Lara admired the floor-to-ceiling Paladian windows and the wall color—a French blue. The tasting bar was marble.

"This is beautiful, Eli! Your sister is very artistic."

"I'll have to admit, she surprised me on this project."

"You still see her as your baby sister," Lara said with amusement.

He gave her a crooked smile. "I suppose I do. It's difficult to see Jillie any other way, but I guess I'm going to have to."

Lara touched the corner of his mouth. "I like it when you smile. Which you do only on rare occasions."

"I've been told I take life too seriously, but I guess it's the way I've been programmed."

"You're too bitter," she said softly, and ran her finger along his cheek. His eyes darkened and he inhaled, reaching for her.

"Give me a reason to be otherwise," he said in a husky voice.

She slipped out of his embrace. "One excellent reason is the delightful party your family is giving. Let's go back to it."

Amusement showed in his expression as he switched off the lights and took her hand again. "First let me show you our horses. Then we'll rejoin everyone."

She walked with him and listened to him talk about wine. They visited the stable and she looked at the lake, the still water shimmering in the late evening. Finally they returned to the party.

They joined Lucas and Caroline again, along with a couple of neighbors. In minutes Caroline recognized a young woman who approached them with a smiling baby in her arms.

"Lara, this is Anna Sheridan," Lucas said. "And this is little Jack. Anna, meet Lara Hunter."

As Lucas made introductions, Jack held his chubby arms out to Lara. She laughed and reached for him.

"You don't have to take him," Anna said, but Lara lifted him into her arms.

"He's adorable," she said, looking into big green eyes as he smiled at her.

"He'll steal your heart," Lucas said. "He's a lovable baby."

"And everyone is spoiling him," Anna stated, but Lucas shook his head.

"You can't spoil that baby. He loves the world and the world loves him," Lucas said. "Watch out, Lara. He likes earrings, too," Lucas said, catching Jack's tiny hand as he played with her thin, gold hoop earring. Jack laughed and held his arms out to Lucas. "Up," he said.

Lucas took him from Lara. "Here's my boy and my ears are safe."

As they stood talking, Lara realized that the man who raised Eli and his siblings must have been a great father to them. Lucas was easygoing and pleasant and she suspected he had none of Spencer's narcissistic ways or high temper. Baby Jack got passed around and finally set on his feet when he wriggled to get down. Anna excused herself and left to follow him through the crowd.

The dinner bell rang and Eli took Lara's arm. "Let's get in the buffet line. I've already spotted our place cards and I know which table we have."

"It's wonderful that your family took in Anna and the baby. I saw her when Lilah turned her away."

"No one in our family would think of turning her away, least of all my mom or dad. And they'd never, ever turn a baby away," Eli said. "I think Anna was desperate when she came here. I hope this is a haven for her and we can protect her and Jack."

"I'm sure you can protect her from the press."

"That's not all. She had some threatening phone calls and she was worried about Jack's safety."

"I'm glad she's here," Lara replied as they got into line at the buffet. They picked up plates and filled them with steaming brisket, thick barbecue sauce, potato salad and buttery, golden ears of corn. Lara found herself seated between Eli and his sister Jillian, whose husband, Seth, and three-year old daughter, Rachel, were on the other side of Jillian. Beside Rachel was a Napa family, the Trents, who had two children. While Eli talked about grapes to Don Trent, Jillian turned to her.

"I'm glad you're here."

"Thanks. It's great to be here," she said to the wavy-haired brunette. Jillian had the family's green eyes.

"You're good for Eli. He's more cheerful tonight." Jillian looked around Lara and saw that her brother was engaged in conversation with Don. She shifted her attention back to Lara. "He's never brought a woman home before."

Lara laughed. "Maybe not, but in this case, it doesn't mean anything. We're just having fun together. Both of us are too busy for anything serious. I'll go to law school in the fall."

"Eli's too busy making wine," Jillian said with a smile.

"I've noticed, but he must be very good at what he does."

"He is," Jillian agreed. "Especially if everyone does things his way," she added, and Lara smiled.

"I heard my name," Eli said, returning his attention to Lara and looking around her at his sister.

"It was complimentary," Lara said, smiling at him.

"I doubt that, if Jillie's involved," he teased, and Jillian wrinkled her nose at him.

While they ate, the sun went down and lights came on across the patio. Lara enjoyed the group at their table and the easy banter among Eli, his sister and brother-in-law.

Later, after dinner, Eli took Lara's hand. "Come upstairs. I want you to see where I live."

She walked at his side, aware of his hand holding hers and their arms brushing. The intimacy of seeing where he lived worried her. It would make saying goodbye even harder. She thought of starting law school in the fall, reminding herself that she needed to keep from getting more entangled with Eli. Once she started school, there would be no place for him in her life. Every moment spent with him now would make that goodbye more difficult. Yet how wonderful the night had been! His family was delightful and friendly. He had been relaxed and attentive, another side to him revealed.

The sounds of music, laughter, people talking and the clink of glasses faded as they entered the empty house, going through the family room decorated in shades of green with comfy sofas and lots of family photos.

"This room looks cozy," Lara said.

"It is, and the family spends a lot of time in here. We used to spend more time here when we were kids. Now everyone is getting scattered. Jillian and Cole are married and have moved out.

Mercedes has her own place. Mason is studying in France. I'm upstairs at one end of the house, and Mom and Dad are downstairs at the other end."

They passed through the covered lanai before entering the formal living room. It was cheerfully decorated and held many antiques.

"Your mother is a wonderful decorator," Lara said.

"It's her magic touch," Eli said, sounding pleased as he held Lara's hand.

Passing through the gallery, they took curving stairs to the second floor where Eli showed her the sitting room and theater with a huge projection screen. More family photos adorned the main hall on the second floor, and she paused to look at them, looking at pictures of Eli when he was a child.

"You have a great family," she said.

"I agree with you," he answered. "Now come see where I live." Eli led her to his suite that was decorated in bright blues and greens, giving it a cheerful air that didn't fit the man who resided there.

"This is great, Eli! It's attractive and masculine. Did your mother do this room?"

"Actually, I picked out some of this, but I took Jillian with me," he said, closing the door behind them. "Here's the kitchenette," he said. Lara stepped into a small room decorated in more festive blues and greens with antique ash cabinets.

"Come see my bedroom," he said, and she glanced at him sharply, but he merely took her hand and led her into a spacious bedroom with a four-poster king-size bed, an ornately carved writing desk and an entertainment center. One wall was lined with shelves, and when she strolled over to look at his books, she saw most of them were on growing grapes or wine production. There were novels, a sizable section of books about France and a few children's books. She touched the spine of a familiar book.

"That was mine when I was a boy," he said from behind her, his breath fanning her ear. He turned her to face him, and the look in his eyes set her heart fluttering.

When he drew her to him, Lara put her hands against his chest to stop him. "Eli, you'll wrinkle my blouse and I'm not returning to your family's party all rumpled."

As she talked, he leaned down to kiss her throat and she felt his fingers deftly unfastening her buttons. "We can take care of that," he whispered.

She pushed again, yet closed her eyes with the onslaught of seductive sensations caused by his feathery kisses. "Eli, we're at a family party. Anyone could come in—"

"Not to my suite. No one will come in, and besides, they're all outside partying. We could be on the moon," he whispered, showering kisses along her throat. He slipped her blouse off and tossed it onto a chair. Pulling her into his arms, he covered her mouth with his and closed his strong arms around her. His tongue explored, tasting, stirring a storm in her. His kiss was deeply possessive, demanding her response. It seduced her, driving all logic and will away. Her heart pounded while she clung to him and responded in kind.

He kissed her as if she were the only woman he had ever known. Moaning softly, ablaze, she thrust her hips against his. She was lost in the storm his kisses created. Passion burned away her logic.

Trembling with longing, she ran her hands down his back and then up over his thick shoulders.

His hand cupped her breast, and through her lacy bra she felt his thumb circle her nipple. Felt it tauten, tingle. She gasped with pleasure, closing her eyes and tightening her arm around his neck. Then his fingers slid to the clasp of her bra. With a flick he unfastened it and shoved away the filmy lace.

Both of his large hands cupped her breasts. His fingers were rough and callused, and the contact was erotic. He stroked her nipples before leaning to use his mouth. His tongue traced one nipple and then he bit it lightly. She cried out with pleasure and wound her fingers through his hair.

"Eli," she whispered, clinging to him, on fire now from his kisses and caresses. She was caught in a flood of longing.

A storm of need shook her. She no longer cared what his family might think they were doing. All she knew was Eli was loving her, and she wanted him intensely.

"You're gorgeous, Lara," he whispered as he laved kisses on first one breast and then another. Her pulse roared and, dimly, she knew his hands were on the zipper of her slacks. Desire was a driving force and all the protective barriers she had wrapped around her were ripped away by the onslaught of his caresses and kisses.

"Eli," she whispered. He nipped at her shoulder and then trailed his tongue to her breast again.

Her slacks fell around her ankles and then his hand was in her panties, caressing her intimately, finding her soft folds and secret places.

Her hands slid over his chest and she discovered he was barechested. She didn't know when he had tossed away his shirt. She tangled her fingers in his chest hair. His fingers built her need. Her caution blew away like leaves in a storm as she clutched his upper arms. Her hips thrust frantically while she sought release. Pressure built, and then she crashed over a brink, hot waves of desire rocking her.

"Eli!" she gasped. She held him tightly while her heartbeat slowed. "We have to stop."

"All right, Lara," he whispered, showering kisses on her face. "I want to love you for hours," he whispered, his tongue tracing the curve of her ear.

She pushed away, bending down to yank up her slacks. With shaking fingers she fastened her slacks and then looked up to find him watching her while he pulled on his shirt and buttoned it. His thick rod pushed against his slacks, his arousal obvious.

"Stop looking at me," she exclaimed, his hungry gaze making her want to walk right back into his embrace.

"You're gorgeous," he said in a raspy voice, "and I could look at you forever."

Aware of his gaze on her that kept her pulse drumming, Lara yanked up her bra to put it on. When he reached out to caress her breast, she drew a sharp breath. "Eli, you have to stop. I can't get emotionally involved with anyone. You don't want to, either."

"It's physical, Lara, and I like being with you."

She shot him a look, wondering if all he wanted was sex. She dressed swiftly. She crossed the bedroom to a cheval mirror and tried to comb her hair with her fingers. He walked up to stand behind her and handed her a comb. "Here's a comb. This may be easier than using your hand."

Wordlessly, she took the comb to fix her hair, thankful she hadn't pinned it up tonight because she would never have gotten it back in place without her hairbrush. He brushed a kiss across her nape.

"Eli," she said solemnly. "We have to get some distance between us."

His hooded eyes regarded her, and she wondered if he knew that her pulse was pounding. He merely nodded as if he had no intention of pursuing her or seducing her.

"Stop worrying. You look just like you did when we left the party. They expect me to show you my suite and the house." He took her hand. "Come sit down and let's just talk. I've had enough socializing with my family and the neighbors.

Before they left the bedroom, he tugged on her hand. "Lara, hold on. I have something I want to get," he said, and crossed the room to open a drawer. He returned and held out a box wrapped in rose paper and tied with a silk rose ribbon.

Startled, she looked up at him when he held it out to her.

"Go ahead. I want you to have it."

She took the box and carefully opened it.

He chuckled. "You can tear the paper. This is going to take all night."

She pushed away the shiny rose paper and lifted a lid on a small box. Nestled inside against blue velvet was a gold filigree necklace.

"Eli, it's gorgeous," she said.

He lifted it out and looked at her. "Can I put it on you?"

"Of course. It's so beautiful! Thank you, but you shouldn't have."

"None of that," he said. "Turn around." As he fastened the necklace, he brushed kisses across her nape, creating tingles. She looked down at the necklace and turned to slide her arms around his neck.

"It's so pretty. It's an antique, isn't it?"

"Yes. I asked Mom if—"

"Eli! I can't take your mother's necklace," she exclaimed, aghast.

"Shh. I asked her if she had one that she didn't wear and I told her you collect antique jewelry. She was happy to let me have it. Believe me, Lara. She doesn't wear it and she was glad to pass it on. It was my grandmother's."

"Eli, you can't do this. Someday you'll get married and your wife should have it."

"She might hate antique jewelry. I want you to have it. End of conversation."

She stared at him a moment and then put her arms around his neck again to kiss him.

He held her tightly, returning her kiss, until she pushed against him. "Eli, if we don't stop, we'll be back where we were just minutes ago."

"And that would be bad?" he asked with an arch in one dark eyebrow. Before she could answer him he took her hand in his again. "Let's get something to drink and talk awhile."

He took her hand to go to his kitchenette. "I have pop, grape juice, wine, iced tea," he said, dropping her hand and looking in his refrigerator.

"Iced tea, please," she said.

In minutes they were seated close together on the sofa in his living room, their drinks on a coffee table in front of them. Eli faced her and played with her hair with one hand while he had his other hand on her knee. "I'm glad you came to the party tonight."

"And I'm glad to meet your friendly family. They've been wonderful."

"I'm proud of them. We've come a long way since Spencer left us. I wish I didn't have one drop of his blood in my veins," Eli said, and a muscle worked in his jaw.

"You shouldn't let old animosities destroy your happiness," Lara said, touching his cheek with her hand and then sliding her fingers to his nape. She wound her fingers in the short strands of his hair above the back of his neck.

Eli ran his hand across his forehead and looked as if he was gazing off in the distance. "I guess all my life I wanted Spencer to acknowledge us and what we accomplished. I saw him twice at wine tastings. He just looked through me like he didn't see me and went on his way."

"I'm so sorry," she said, hurting for Eli. She ran her fingers over his hand that rested on her knee.

"I guess there's that eight-year-old-kid still in me that wanted some kind of recognition from him," Eli said. "Damn him, anyway."

"Let it go, Eli. Spencer isn't worth agonizing over. I don't know who the killer was, but I'm glad Spencer is gone."

Eli's gaze swung to her and his eyes narrowed. "What did he do to you? I can just imagine—you're beautiful, Lara. That bastard tried to seduce you, didn't he?"

Eight

"**I** think he tried to seduce every female under forty who looked even remotely appealing. He threatened to fire my mother if I didn't cooperate with him," Lara said with distaste.

"Damn! You—"

"I didn't give in to him. But he threatened often enough, and it was just another reason to hate the man." She shivered. "He was a beast."

"The killer probably had a lot of reasons for pulling the trigger," Eli said.

"The first suspect was Charlotte because she found his body, but thank goodness she has an alibi—she was with Alexandre Dupree. Even so, Alexandre was going to take her to France, and now they can't go. The police won't let her leave the country."

"It's a good thing a lot of us have alibis," Eli said, brushing his fingers back and forth on Lara's nape. She inhaled deeply, tingling from his caresses, wondering if he was even aware of what he was doing or if he noticed her fingers tangled in his hair. "I'm known for my temper—which I inherited from him, I'll have to admit. I told you that I was with one of our workers and I'm glad I have an alibi because people know the animosity I felt for Spencer."

"The detectives questioned everyone at the estate. Several of us on the staff were playing cards," Lara said. "I'm thankful I have an alibi because I don't think it would be wise to have it come out how much I disliked Spencer," she said.

"I want to see if we can break Spencer's will," Eli revealed bluntly. "My family disagrees with me."

"I've heard rumors since the reading of the will. Rumors about all the Ashtons constantly fly through the staff. Of course, you may have a legitimate cause," she said. Lara thought about the Ashtons and how shocked they would be if Eli and his family did contest the will.

"You look worried," he said, one dark eyebrow climbing, and she heard the bitterness creep back into his voice.

"People continually disappoint you, don't they, Eli?" she asked, knowing he was hurting and indignant over Spencer's will.

"I suppose your sympathies lie with the other Ashtons."

"I was just thinking how it will rock their world if the will is contested. And it'll come in a year when they have had one scandal after another hit them."

"Thanks to Spencer," Eli snapped.

"That's true, but Megan and Paige and the others were as innocent as your family."

He inhaled and looked away, and his fingers stilled in her hair. "Walker Ashton shouldn't inherit my grandfather's stock," Eli insisted, his voice laced with anger.

Lara hurt for Eli and placed her hand against his cheek. His gaze returned to hers and he turned his head to kiss her palm. His hand covered hers and held her palm to his lips while his tongue traced a circle in the center of her hand. As tingles radiated from his kiss, she forgot families and wills. All Lara wanted was to be in his arms again. And she saw the same desire in the depths of his eyes.

"Lara," he sighed, pulling her onto his lap to cradle her against his shoulder and kiss her deeply. Lara wound an arm around his neck to return his kisses. Once again she was caught in the dizzying spiral of his kisses. Desire escalated, threatening to shatter the control she had fought to keep.

Finally she pushed away from him and stood. "Oh, Eli. I'm wrinkled."

"Your blouse has a few wrinkles. It's night. No one will notice."

"Of course they'll notice. Your patio has lights. We should join the others."

Standing, he framed her face with his hands. "I want you, Lara. I want you in my arms. I want you in my life."

"We both got carried away that one night. It mustn't happen again."

His eyelids drooped and fires danced in the depths of his eyes. His arm tightened around her waist and he leaned forward, pulling her against his chest. His mouth came down on hers hard and his tongue went into her mouth, kissing her possessively, melting her opposition. He kissed her until she wound her arms around his neck and returned his kisses.

He swung her up. Bemused, she opened her eyes to look up at him, and she knew how thoroughly he had proved his point that he would get his way.

She shook her head. "Doesn't matter what you do tonight. I'm not going to be seduced. And I should go. It's late and I don't want to go down and find everyone except your family has gone. Worse, I don't want to come out of your suite as your family is coming inside to go to bed."

"Mom and Dad have rooms at the other end of the house on the ground floor. No one else is around. Mason's room is the closest and he's in France."

"Let's go, Eli," she insisted, and he draped his arm across her shoulders.

"Whatever you want," he said.

The party was still going when they went downstairs, but a few guests were beginning to leave. After another half hour, Lara told Eli that she should go, so they said goodbye to everyone and she thanked his mother and father for the evening.

As they left the lights and the party, Eli drew her to his side.

He gave her a crooked smile. "My family liked you," Eli said as they walked to his car.

"Of course they did. You finally brought home a woman. And it sounds as if they like everybody."

"Oh, no. They would let me know if they didn't like you. No one is fond of Craig Bradford, Mercedes's on-again, off-again boyfriend. But then, I don't think Mercedes is that fond of him, either. No, you'd know. They like you."

"It was a great party," she said, wanting to get away from the discussion of his family liking her. She was returning to her plain life, and she didn't want to dwell too much on the evening.

Eli held the car door for her and in minutes they were on the highway, heading south to the Ashton Estate. When Eli parked near her door, he cut the motor and turned to her. "I'm glad you came tonight. Let me take you to dinner tomorrow night."

"I had a wonderful time at the party and I enjoyed meeting your family," she said carefully, her heart beating fast. "Eli, we might as well say goodbye right now. I've told you, I have plans, and our going out together is no part of them."

"If I thought you didn't like me, I'd say fine and leave you alone," he said in a low voice. "But I know differently. When we're together your heartbeat is as out of control as mine. There's a chemistry between us that is as combustible as a flash fire. You have plans, but you told me they're for the fall. What's it going to hurt to go out tomorrow night?"

"Every hour we're together makes saying goodbye more complicated, and you know I'm right. We're not going out again," she said forcefully and stepped out of the car swiftly. She ran and almost made it to the door before he caught her. He spun her around and they looked at each other.

"No," she whispered.

"You say no. Your heart says yes."

"This time you're not going to change my mind. Until you came into my life I've always had control over my emotions and I'm not going to lose that control."

"You're fighting yourself right now," he remarked.

"You act as if you can't hear a word I'm saying to you. Eli, this is goodbye. And if you say one word, then you're more like Spencer than you want to admit. He had—"

"Dammit. Maybe I'm not worthy of your love, but stop accusing me of being like Spencer!" Eli snapped.

His words stopped her cold. "Love?" Lara looked at him searchingly. "Eli, what—"

Eli was angry now. "Never mind. It was a stupid slip of the tongue. It didn't mean a thing—nothing at all."

Lara knew what he really meant: he was reminding her that

although their time together had been magical, it was still insignificant to him. She turned and pushed buttons to unlock the door. The moment she did, she stepped inside and slammed it behind her. She was gasping for breath and she hurt.

She clenched her fists and wished she had been able to control her emotions. All her life she had been able to keep a cool head, but with Eli she couldn't. She suspected she was testing his restraint, too, but if it had taken that to get him to listen to her, so be it. Yet his words broke her heart. Even though she knew what they'd shared was temporary, hearing Eli's angry words tonight had hurt. And he wasn't like Spencer—not in the ways that really counted.

She headed for the stairs in the silent house, climbing them and thinking about the party that had been so wonderful. The night had been enchanted, and she reflected on the moments in Eli's arms, his kisses that she knew she could never forget. In her small room she closed the door and let the tears come, because in her heart she didn't want to tell him goodbye.

A light tap on the door made her wipe frantically at her tears. She glanced at her clock. It was past midnight. She swung open the door, thankful she no longer had to worry about Spencer. Franci stood there in striped orange-and-black pajamas and an orange cotton robe. She waved a tray of cheese and crackers and two bottles of pop.

"I can't sleep and I wanted to hear about your evening."

"Franci, do you know how late it is?"

"Are you going to sleep now?"

"No," Lara admitted and swung open the door. Franci sailed inside and plopped on the bed, placing the food on the small bedside table. "I'll fix the cheese and crackers while you get ready for bed and tell me. Did you have an exciting evening?"

"I had a wonderful time," Lara said solemnly, and Franci looked up, her eyes narrowing.

"You've been crying. Did you fight with him?"

Lara sighed, knowing Franci was her best friend and that sooner or later, Franci would learn what had happened. "I told him I won't go out with him again."

"Why?" Franci shrieked and then clamped her hands over her mouth.

"Shh! You'll wake up the house. And I don't want Mom asking me a million questions and discussing this with the entire staff."

"You like him. Why on earth would you tell him you won't go out? Franci asked, kicking off fluffy orange slippers and sitting cross-legged on the bed while Lara changed to yellow cotton pajamas. She emerged to hang up her blouse and slacks. "I have to stop before things get out of hand," she said woodenly. She crossed the room to the bed to find Franci staring at her.

"You're in love with him!" Franci exclaimed, wriggling with excitement and making her thick mop of black curls bounce.

"No, I'm not!"

"Yes, you are," Franci argued. "You're in love! Why won't you go out with him if you're in love?"

Lara thought about Franci's accusation. Was she in love with Eli? "I may have fallen in love with him, Franci, but he just seems to want a physical relationship. And he seems to be so singleminded."

"Give it up a little. Give him a chance," Franci said, slicing cheese and putting it on a cracker. Lara shook her head.

"I can't eat a bite."

"Oh, my. You're definitely in love. You always have a little snack with me when I bring one to your room. No appetite, tears. Go out with the man and follow your heart."

Lara shook her head, hating her churning emotions and the threat of more tears. She took off the necklace Eli had given her and turned it in her hands. "He gave me this because he knows I like antique jewelry. It was his grandmother's."

"He loves you, too!"

"No, he doesn't. It's a bauble to him. I'm going to mail it back to him tomorrow."

"You can't, Lara! Stop tossing away happiness with both hands, for heavens sake!"

"I have to do what I have to do," Lara said, placing the necklace on her dresser.

"Okay. Tell me about his family. Are any of them overbearing like Spencer?"

"Eli is probably the one who is most like Spencer, but he'd hate to hear me say that. No, they're not. They're wonderful people and I had a marvelous time. Franci, I hurt him tonight. I told him that he was like Spencer and he got so angry. I just need to take care of Mom and go to law school, and I don't have a place for a man in my life right now."

"You're in love and you have to go out with him again."

"No, I don't," Lara said woodenly, and in minutes she claimed a headache and shooed Franci out of her room, sagging against the door with relief when she was alone. She switched off the light and climbed into bed, but memories of that first night with Eli plagued her. He didn't belong in her life, and the more she saw him, the bigger the heartbreak would be. And heartbreak would come. Eli didn't want any commitment. She had a plan for her life to follow and there was no place for Eli in her plan.

Yet his words haunted her. *Maybe I'm not worthy of your love, but stop accusing me of being like Spencer!* Lara wondered if it had really been a slip of the tongue. Could Eli have fallen in love with her? Did he really think he was unworthy of love because Spencer had abandoned him as a boy? Her heart broke anew.

She balled her fists against her eyes and hated that she couldn't govern her feelings. "Eli," she whispered. "Eli, I love you."

Eli drove home and took the stairs two at a time to go to his suite. He closed the door and walked to the bedroom, tossing off his clothes, throwing them over a chair. He paced the room and felt on fire. He wanted Lara and she didn't want to go out again—and it wasn't because she didn't like him. Her reasons frustrated him and he tried not to be angry. Worst of all, he'd said the *L* word—which he didn't understand at all. Where had *that* come from? She'd just got him so riled.

"Damnation," he said, raking his fingers through his hair. He spun around and went to his closet. In minutes he was dressed to swim. Leaving the house, he crossed the yard and headed to the lake. He switched a light on, on one tall pole along the dock at the lake. It threw a shimmering silver beam across the inky water. He dropped his towel and kicked off his loafers, making a running dive into the cold water.

He swam until he was nearly exhausted and finally climbed out, toweling off and slipping back into his shoes. He turned off the light and walked through the vineyard to go back to the house.

Picking a grape leaf, Eli rubbed his fingers over it, feeling the texture. His thoughts jumped right back to Lara and her kisses. She'd had a good time tonight. "Forget her," he told himself, striding back to his suite where he uncorked a bottle of Merlot and poured a drink. He sat in his living room, thinking about being there with her hours ago. He wanted her in his arms. He wanted her in his bed. He glanced at his bedroom and, for the first time in years, thought about getting an apartment in Napa. He wanted his own place.

He raked his fingers through his hair. "Dammit," he mumbled. Even if he had his own place, she wouldn't stay with him. She was a woman with a plan that didn't include him. He had to forget her, but she wouldn't stay out of his thoughts.

He had to respect her plans to take care of her mother. From the time he was eight until Louret became a success, Eli's whole purpose in life was to take care of his mom and his siblings. He and Lara were alike in that, and he admired Lara for it. And he admired her independence—so long as she didn't direct it toward him.

She wasn't like any woman he had ever known. Independent, poised, driven—and sexy beyond measure.

He took a long drink and lowered the glass, staring into space and seeing Lara, thinking about her light-brown eyes and her thick auburn lashes. remembering holding her in his arms, dancing with her. Another disappointment in a lifetime of disappointments and rejection. And Lara wondered why he didn't trust people.

He rubbed his forehead. *Was* he in love? Had he ever been in knots before, even when he had been in serious relationships? He'd been hurt, but not as though his heart had been ripped out.

He groaned and, like an animal in a cage, got up to pace the room. His tall clock chimed three. He strode through his suite and dressed in chinos and a knit shirt and left again, heading to his office. He knew he wasn't going to sleep, so, hopefully, if he threw himself into work, he would forget her for a while.

Over a week later, on the twenty-second of June, Eli stood,

brushed dirt off his work pants and climbed back on a tractor. He had been plowing under their winter cover crop of barley and legumes that had been planted between the rows of vines. He glanced at his watch and saw that it was four-thirty in the afternoon. As he reached toward the ignition, his cell phone rang. Eli pulled it out of his pocket and answered, "Eli, here."

"It's Grant."

Eli frowned because Grant's voice had an unfamiliar rasp to it. Instantly he suspected a problem. "What's wrong?" Eli asked.

"Two detectives from the SFPD are here," Grant replied in a tight voice, and Eli's stomach clenched. "They're taking me in for questioning," Grant added.

"Damn!" Eli swore. Concern for Grant's welfare mushroomed because Grant didn't have an alibi and, worse, he had a motive. Yet Eli didn't think Grant could have committed the murder any more than he himself could have. "I'm in the vineyards right now and I'm hot and dirty, but I can be ready soon. Will they let me ride into the city with you?"

"I'll ask," Grant said, and Eli could hear muted voices before Grant returned to the phone. "No. I have to go alone with them. At least there are no handcuffs so far."

"Have you told Mom or Dad? "

"No. You're the only person I've called. I'm still here at Louret," Grant said. "I asked them if I could clean up and change clothes. They said I could."

"I'll clean up and get there as soon as possible," Eli said. "You need a lawyer. The family will take care of it."

"Thank God for your family! Tell your folks thanks until I can tell them myself. I'm glad you're coming. It'll be reassuring to have someone with me."

"You wait for an attorney to get there before you answer any questions. I'm on my way." Eli jammed his phone in his pocket, started the tractor and headed home. He dreaded breaking the news to Lucas and Caroline because he knew they were fond of Grant and would be upset. His mother answered the phone in a friendly voice.

"Mom, I've got bad news." Eli tried to cushion what he had to say, pausing a moment. "Grant just called and the detectives are taking him in for questioning."

"Eli, that's horrible! You know Grant wouldn't have shot Spencer," Caroline exclaimed.

"I know, but as far as the police are concerned, he had a motive."

"A lot of people had motives. We'll hire a lawyer for Grant. I'll see if I can get Ridley Pollard to recommend an experienced criminal attorney," Caroline said. "You call Grant and tell him we'll have a lawyer meet him in the city."

"Thanks, Mom."

Minutes later he raced up the stairs to his suite. As soon as he closed his door, he yanked off his clothes and tossed them down as he rushed to shower. He was toweling dry when his cell phone rang again.

It was Lucas. "Eli, the attorney for Grant is Edgar Kent, and Ridley will go along with him for moral support. Are you going into town?"

"Yes. I'm dressing as fast as I can."

"Keep in touch. Someone's at the door so I have to go."

Eli yanked on a burnt-orange knit shirt and dark-brown slacks. As he was jamming his feet into his loafers his phone rang again. Expecting another call from Grant, Eli answered. Instead of Grant, he heard his dad.

"Eli, Detective Holbrook is here at the house," Lucas announced, and Eli closed his eyes. He knew from Lucas's tone that bad news was coming. "The detective is taking your mother in for questioning, too."

Eli turned to ice and clenched his fist. "What? Where are you?"

"We're still at the house. She's getting her things."

"Dammit to hell!" Eli swore. "Will they let you ride with Mom?"

"Yes," Lucas answered. "We're leaving now. I've already called Ridley Pollard back to get another criminal lawyer for Mom. We don't want to take the one away from Grant."

"Will you be in an unmarked car?"

"Yes. It's a black four-door sedan with antennae all over it," Lucas remarked dryly. "We won't be hard to spot, and I'll be with her. There are two detectives and they're in plain clothes."

"How's Mom?"

"She's fine. She didn't shoot Spencer, and she said she had no reason to. Maybe when all of you were babies, but not now. She's calm about the whole thing because she's certain of her innocence. Besides, she was home with me that night, but that didn't satisfy them because I left for a brief time. We have to go in," Lucas said in such a soft voice that Eli could barely hear him.

"Sure," Eli said. "I'll call the others. Everyone has gone home for the day. I wondered if the detectives waited for that to happen."

"I don't know. Let's just pray the press doesn't get wind of this. Goodbye, Eli," Lucas said.

Eli broke the connection. He hadn't thought about the press. The tabloids would feed on this latest development.

He swore as he pulled on his belt and combed his hair. He jogged to the garage, flinging himself into the car. His mother.

How could they haul his mother in for questioning? And just as she said, if she'd ever harbored murderous intentions toward Spencer, why wait thirty years to do it—when she was happily married and Louret Winery was a huge success.

"Dammit!" Eli swore again as he jammed his foot on the accelerator and took off down the drive with a squeal of tires.

He yanked out his phone, breaking his own rule about not using the phone while the car was moving. He called his siblings to inform them, getting Cole and Jillian but unable to locate Mercedes. He called Jillian back to tell her, and she said she would continue trying to get Mercedes.

Louret Vineyards to San Francisco was an hour-and-a-half drive, but within twenty-five minutes Eli spotted the police car ahead of him on the highway. He eased up on the accelerator and gradually passed the unmarked sedan. When Eli saw his mother and Lucas in the back, he hurt all over at the thought of his gentle mother being questioned by the police.

He thought about Anna and how she had fled from the press. Would the press already know about Caroline and Grant?

Eli clamped his jaw closed until it hurt. If there were reporters waiting, he would smash every camera he could get his hands on. "Right, Eli," he told himself, knowing if he tore into the press, his actions would ensure front-page coverage. He hit the steering wheel with his fist. His mother hauled in like a criminal—suspected of murder. His gentle mother who was kind to everyone and had given shelter to Grant, Anna and Jack and constantly did things for others.

When his cell phone rang, Eli answered to hear Anna's voice.

"Eli, I heard about Caroline and Grant. Jillian said the police want to question them both," Anna said, sounding alarmed.

"That's right. I'm on my way to San Francisco now. I passed

Mom and Dad so I'll get there before they do and I think Grant and the other detectives are behind Mom and Dad. I should get there before any of them."

"Thank goodness! Please let me know about them. I can't imagine—"

"I'll call you, Anna, as soon as I know something," Eli promised.

"Thanks, Eli." She hung up and Eli tossed down his phone. His stomach was in knots.

While the sun moved lower in the western sky, Eli raced down the highway, finally tearing across the Golden Gate Bridge and heading to the police station, still in shock and disbelief at the latest turn of events. Another scandal to rock the Ashtons! More lurid notoriety that essentially had been caused by Spencer!

When Eli turned into the parking lot of the San Francisco Police Department, he swore again. Two television vans were parked by the door. A man stood leaning against the building, and Eli suspected he was a member of the press. A woman in a white blouse sat in a car. Nearby two men stood talking beside two cars, and Eli guessed they all were reporters waiting for Caroline and Grant to appear.

Eli clamped his jaw closed tightly, knowing the best he could do when his family arrived was get on one side of his mother and let Lucas stay on the other and try to get her into the building without too much hassle from the reporters. But he hated that the story would be in the papers and on television. He watched two men get out of a television van and lift out cameras and equipment. Another cameraman was already set up near the door. Hopefully, the detectives would help and not add to the problem.

A car like the one Lara drove turned into the lot. Eli stared at it grimly. A woman in a floppy hat and dark sunglasses was behind the wheel, and he shifted his attention back to the street to watch for the arrival of the car with his mother.

Since he hadn't spotted Grant on the way to the city, he guessed Grant was farther behind and would come after Caroline and Lucas arrived.

The car like Lara's pulled alongside Eli, and he frowned. He didn't want anyone to get in his way. When he looked at the woman, she motioned to him. Startled, he frowned and took a harder look. His stomach clenched.

Nine

Lara got out of her car and slid into his, closing the door.

"What are you doing here?" he asked sharply, stunned to see her. He ached to pull her into his arms.

Her bright red, Look-at-me! suit had a matching red silk blouse. She wore high-heeled red pumps on her feet. The hat that framed her face was a perfect background for her peaches-and-cream skin. While his mouth went dry and his pulse pounded, he wanted to reach for her and pull her into his arms. Instead, he kept his hands to himself and tried to listen to what she was telling him.

"I was in town and heard on the news that the police intend to question your mother about Spencer's murder. I figured you'd be here and thought I'd see if I could help in any way," she said.

"I didn't recognize you at first," he replied, looking at her floppy hat and the dark sunglasses. He couldn't see her eyes, and the hat hid her hair and part of her face.

"If the press gets my picture, I don't want to be recognizable."

"Your red suit practically screams for attention, and everyone will notice you," he said roughly. The urge to pull her hat off and run his fingers through her hair grew by the minute, but he controlled his impulse.

"I came to the city three hours ago. I can't do anything now about my suit. This is an old hat I had tossed into the back of the car."

"I think the reporters will focus on my family, but if you get out of the car, you'll be on the news with us," he said, his mind only half on their conversation, the rest of his thoughts swirling over Lara. Why was she here?

"That's what I figured. Lilah Ashton would be less than happy to find I'm here to support your family at this moment. Where is your mother?"

"I passed them on the way here. They should arrive any minute now. The police intend to question Grant, too."

Lara nodded. "That's on the news."

"Damn, I hate this," Eli grumbled. "I hate it for both of them. Our lives have been one crisis after another, and this last year has been pure hell. It's not the first time, but I think we've had more than our share of trouble. Always the turmoil goes back to Spencer. He couldn't even die without tormenting us."

Lara squeezed Eli's hand, and he focused on her. "If you don't want Lilah Ashton to know you're here with us, you better leave," he said, still surprised that Lara had come. She seemed cool and remote, and he suspected her presence didn't mean her feelings toward him had changed, but at the moment he couldn't sort it out. Right now he was in knots about his mother and Grant.

"There are already two television crews here, and I'm sure

there are three reporters. Here comes another damned reporter," he said when a woman drove into the parking lot. "Lara, don't jeopardize yourself. Dad and I are here, and the others are on their way."

"I'm not too recognizable. My face is almost covered and I don't wear this hat at the estate. I want to be here, Eli."

Her words strummed across his heart. She *wanted* to be with him and his family. Was it pity? Sympathy? Or something deeper? How much did she care?

It was tempting to tell her to get in her car and go because now there were two women he wanted to shield from the media instead of concentrating on one. Yet deep down, in spite of her aloofness, he was glad to see her and he couldn't send her away.

Her perfume stirred vivid memories of Lara in his arms, Lara pressed close against him. He wiped his brow while he watched a long, dark-green car whip into the lot and park. Three men climbed out, all dressed in dark suits and all of them carrying briefcases. They hurried toward the building to disappear inside.

"Thank God, there go our lawyers!" Eli exclaimed.

"Do you want to let them know you're here?"

"No, they knew I was on my way. That tall, black-haired one is Ridley Pollard, our family attorney, and he's here for moral support. The other two are criminal lawyers he recommended. I haven't met them yet. Mom hired Edgar Kent for Grant."

"Your mother has the proverbial heart of gold."

"Yes, she does. I want to wait for Mom and Dad so I can help Dad shield her from the press as she goes into the building."

"When you mother arrives, I'll go with you. I'll just be another person to keep reporters away from her."

"Here they come," he said, watching the unmarked sedan pull into the lot. The television crews jumped into action, running toward the car with their cameras already going. As the reporters gathered, Eli stepped out of the car. When Lara joined him, he took her arm, and they rushed to the official car. Eli merely nodded at Detective Holbrook whose blue eyes were impassive behind her glasses. Eli didn't know the other tall, thin detective.

Keeping Lara at his side, Eli shouldered his way past a reporter. He knew a television cameraman was filming every second. Caroline emerged from the car. She looked stylish in a black suit and a black silk shirt, but she was pale and visibly trembling, which sent Eli's anger soaring. Only a few feet in front of her a flash went off and then another one while other cameras whirred.

As Eli moved close to her right side, the detectives stepped in front. Lucas had his arm around her waist on her left and they all walked together. Eli glanced over his shoulder to see Lara directly behind Caroline as she said she would be.

There was no way to totally shield Caroline, Eli thought as reporters crowded in, taking pictures and shouting questions. A microphone was jammed in front of Eli, and he heard questions that were aimed at him, but he had no intention of answering. Furious, he reached out to grab the camera, but Lara caught his arm, and he held back. Simmering with anger, he knew he should control his temper.

Suddenly a television cameraman got through, shoving the camera in Caroline's face as he shouted questions at her.

Eli's temper exploded, and he grabbed the camera. For an instant there was a tug-of-war between the two men, but Eli yanked, and the camera slipped out of the newsman's hands. Eli tossed the camera to the ground and it smashed against the asphalt, pieces splattering.

Several of the newsmen shouted at Eli, but he ignored them.

He could hear one of them yelling at the detectives to arrest Eli. Instead, the detectives walked faster, and Eli and Lucas hurried Caroline along.

"You'll have to pay for my camera!" came a shout behind Eli.

The thirty yards to the door seemed a mile, but then the detectives were there. The man held open the door, and Detective Holbrook stepped back to block the reporters.

Caroline and her entourage swept inside, and Detective Holbrook closed the door. Eli looked down at Caroline. They strode down a hall into a room that held a desk with a sergeant on duty and another desk with a dispatcher. Detective Holbrook led them through a closed door into a large waiting room.

"No reporters will be allowed in here," she said.

Chairs lined one side of the plain room, with a drinking fountain on the other side. A low rail divided the area from another room filled with desks. Eli barely noticed his surroundings as he looked down at his mother.

"You okay?" he asked, and she patted his arm, but she was paler than before, and he knew the past few seconds from the car to the station had been upsetting to her.

"Thanks for being here." She turned around. "Lara, thank you, too."

"I'm glad to help in any little way," Lara replied, and Caroline squeezed Lara's hand.

The three attorneys joined them, and Ridley Pollard introduced Edgar Kent and Amos Detmer to all of the Ashtons and Lara.

"Ridley, you may have to bail Eli out now," Caroline said, giving a worried glance to her oldest son. The attorney nodded his head and turned to Eli. "I'll talk to the cameraman. He may have already contacted his attorney."

"Thanks," Eli said, all his worries focused on Caroline. At the moment he wasn't concerned with the reporter.

Detective Holbrook had stepped to the desk, but she returned. "Mrs. Sheppard, if you'll please come with me."

It was a nightmare for Eli—a moment he never expected to see. He wanted to fling himself between his mother and the detectives, but he knew he'd only make things worse. He let out a long breath. Also, he wanted to hug his mother, but there wasn't a chance. Lucas gave her a quick hug and stepped back as Amos Detmer moved to her side.

Lucas looked over his shoulder. "Eli, thanks for all your help. You're sticking around, aren't you?"

"Yes. Grant isn't here yet."

"Watch for him. The reporters will swamp him." Lucas glanced at Lara, and his eyebrows arched. "Lara," he greeted her. "It was good of you to come be with us."

"Hello, Mr. Sheppard," she said, removing her sunglasses. "I'm sorry this happened."

"Thanks. We'll get it sorted out, and the truth will prevail," Lucas said calmly. "We might as well sit down, because I'm guessing this is going to take some time." He walked away, leaving Eli and Lara alone.

"I'll wait outside for Grant," Eli told her, unable to resist touching her as he brushed a tendril of auburn hair away from her cheek.

"You won't want the reporters questioning you," she reminded him. "They watched you walk in with your mother, so now they'll have a hundred questions for you," Lara said. "They're unhappy with you at the moment, anyway."

"You're right. I don't want to tangle with them. I probably didn't help Mom or my family. I guess I'll stay inside."

"I can't go out without questions, either, because they don't know who I am. As we came in here, several reporters asked my name and how I know the family. One asked me if my name was Anna Sheridan."

"Well, hell. I guess we just sit tight and let Grant fend for himself." Eli studied her and thought she looked thinner. "You shouldn't have gotten involved."

She shrugged. "It's dreadful that the police suspect your mother."

"It's ridiculous. If she intended to shoot Spencer, she would have done it when he left us. Not now." Eli pulled out his cell phone. "I'm going to call Cole, Jillian and Mercedes and tell them to park somewhere else, that the back lot is filled with media. I'll be with you in a minute."

"Take your time," Lara replied, and waited quietly while he made his calls. When he finished, Eli looked over her head. "Ridley Pollard is back. Excuse me a minute while I see what he learned."

Eli walked away, talking briefly with their stocky, blue-eyed attorney and then returning to Lara while Ridley Pollard sat down with Lucas and Edgar Kent.

"Ridley's going to contact the television station and tell them I'll buy a new camera and see if he can head off charges being filed against me," Eli told Lara.

"I'm sorry all of you are going through this," Lara said.

His gaze went past her. "Here's Grant. Just a minute and I'll be back." He left Lara to greet his half brother, shaking hands with Grant and clasping him on the shoulder. "Mom is already here." Eli said as he shook Grant's hand. Eli merely nodded at Detective Dan Ryland and the other detective who accompanied Grant. The detectives stepped away to go to the desk and talk briefly with the officer on duty. Looking grim, Grant turned his attention to Eli.

"Thanks, Eli, for coming. It means a lot," he said. "Hi, Lara," he added, calling and waving to her.

"Cole is coming, too," Eli said. "I think they all may be here except Mercedes. As far as I know no one has been able to get in touch with her."

Grant said, "I really appreciate everything all of you are doing."

"Anna wanted to know about you and Mom. She called me." Edgar Kent came forward and Eli introduced him, walking away so the two men could confer.

In another minute Detective Ryland joined Grant and the attorney. "Will you come with us," he said, and Grant and Edgar Kent turned to follow the detective.

Eli held Lara's arm. "We might as well sit down unless you want me to try to get you back to your car without too much hassle."

"No. I'll wait with you."

"Here comes my brother," Eli announced, seeing Cole come through a door on the opposite side of the room. Eli waved to Cole and Dixie, who strode toward them. "My practical businessman brother," Eli said, looking at Cole. "He'll be as lost in this situation as I am. There's nothing either of us can do for Mom or Grant now except give moral support."

Dressed in brown slacks and a tan shirt, Cole came forward. While he greeted Lucas and Ridley Pollard first, Eli waited and then greeted his brother and sister-in-law. Eli thought again that Cole had married a beautiful woman. Dixie wore a brightly patterned shirt and green slacks. Her straight, dark-blond hair had a silky sheen and she smiled at Lara and Eli.

"It's nice to see you, Lara. Thanks for lending your support," Cole said.

"Mom and Grant have already been taken somewhere for questioning," Eli said. "An attorney named Amos Detmer is with Mom. Edgar Kent is with Grant."

"Great," Cole remarked. "I guess we just wait. We've been listening to the news. You attacked a cameraman."

"That didn't take long to become news. I smashed his camera. I didn't attack him. He jammed a camera in Mom's face and yelled questions at her," Eli said, and Cole nodded.

"Under those circumstances I might have done the same thing. Have you talked to Ridley Pollard about it?"

"Yes. He's already been on the phone with the television station trying to keep them from pressing assault charges against me."

"That's all we need," Cole said grimly, rubbing the back of his head. "I can't believe this is happening."

"I feel the same way," Eli said. "Mom looked pale and I know she has to be upset."

"We might as well sit down," Cole suggested, turning toward the chairs and taking Dixie's arm.

As soon as they were all seated in the hard, brown wooden chairs that were worn and scarred from use, Lara turned to Eli. "Your family is here now. I'm going to leave."

"Reporters will be all over you," Eli said. "They saw you come in with us." He turned to his brother. "Where are you parked, Cole?"

"Like you told me. Down the street. No one paid any attention to us."

"Lara, give Dixie your car keys. They won't know Dixie, and she can drive your car out of the parking lot to the street. We'll go out the front," Eli said. "Cole, do you want to stay here in case Grant or Mom need us?"

"Sure," Cole replied. "Unless you want me to come with you," he said to Dixie, but she shook her head.

Eli held Lara's arm and looked over her head at Cole. "I'll be back."

Lara told Cole, Lucas and Ridley Pollard goodbye and walked out with Eli. At the door she turned to him and pulled her hat lower. Eli put his arm across her shoulders and they left the building.

"There's no one out here," she exclaimed in surprise, and Eli let out his breath in relief.

"Thank God!" Eli exclaimed. "Cole said there wasn't any press here when he and Dixie arrived."

Eli and Lara went down steps and walked to the drive from the parking lot. "Here comes Dixie with your car." Eli turned to face Lara, dropping his arm from her shoulders. She tilted her head, looking up at him from beneath the wide hat brim. She had the dark glasses on again and he couldn't see her eyes.

"Thanks for coming," he said. "The whole family appreciates it. It'll mean a lot to Mom and Grant."

"I don't know about that," Lara replied. "I was glad to be here and give any support I could. I'm just sorry they're being questioned. I'm sure it'll be in the news how things turn out."

"I'll let you know. Actually, Grant is the one I'm worried about. He had a big motive and no alibi. Dad was with Mom and they ought to get that straightened out quickly. We've got excellent lawyers."

"Here's Dixie. Goodbye, Eli," Lara said.

He wanted to see her again, but he knew she would refuse. It was a situation that was only headed for disappointment. He watched her walk around and get in her car and heard her thank Dixie.

While he stood watching, she drove away, and he wondered if she were driving out of his life forever. Dixie joined him to go back inside. "That was supportive of her, Eli."

"Yeah," he said. "Even so, there weren't enough of us to help get Mom inside without a reporter getting in her face. The reporters and the cameramen mobbed us."

"I'm surprised one isn't stationed around here at this door."

"They probably think everyone goes in the other way," he replied, his thoughts still on Lara. He held the door for Dixie, and as he started inside he glanced around to see Jillian and Seth approaching. "Go on," he told Dixie. "Here comes Jillian and Seth, and I'll wait for them."

He stood at the top of the steps, his thoughts in turmoil over Lara's appearance and Caroline and Grant being questioned. Once again, as he watched his sister and brother-in-law approach holding hands, he was reminded of the void in his own life. He missed Lara every second of every day.

As soon as Jillian and Seth joined him, his sister looked at him with curiosity in her green eyes. "Didn't I see Lara drive away?"

"Yes, you did," he said, holding the door for them and following them inside. "She heard about Mom and Grant."

"I wasn't certain whether it was her or not. She had on a big hat. I thought you said you weren't going to see each other again."

"She wasn't here long," he said, and Jillian turned away to talk to Cole and Dixie. "Mercedes will be here soon," Jillian said.

Eli joined the others as they sat down, but in minutes he got up to pace the floor. He couldn't keep his mind on their conversation. As he stood gazing out a window, Lucas joined him. "Stop worrying, Eli. The police don't have any hard evidence, and they sure won't have anything to tie your mother to it. Or Grant."

"Except motive for Grant. Although, if it were based solely on motive, there would be a hundred other suspects. Spencer had enemies everywhere," Eli said.

"Stop worrying, son," Lucas said, and walked back to join the others.

Eli raked his fingers through his hair. In minutes he heard everyone greet Mercedes, and he turned to say hello to his sister. Her light-brown hair was fastened on top of her head and she wore chic yellow slacks and a striped yellow-and-white cotton blouse. She crossed the room to Eli.

"How's Mom?"

"She's fine, I guess. She was when she left with the detectives."

"They can't hold her. They don't have any evidence to tie her to Spencer's murder," Mercedes said.

"There isn't anything that we know about."

"You know there's nothing to tie Mom to Spencer's murder. I spoke to Ridley. Cole told me he's making phone calls to get you out of hot water. He said you smashed a camera."

"The guy was right in Mom's face."

"I'm glad you did it, but I hope you don't have to go to court over it. Or jail," she added.

"Ridley will take care of the situation, and I'll pay. I don't think I'll have to go to court, although at the rate the Ashtons have been making headlines, I may have to."

"Thanks for getting here as quickly as you did," Mercedes said. "I know Mom and Dad were glad to have you here. Grant, too. I'm sorry you couldn't get hold of me. I left my phone in the car instead of my purse when I was running errands in Napa."

"That's okay." He looked over her head. "That didn't take long. Here's Mom."

"Eli, she looks as if she's going to faint," Mercedes said with a frown.

"Dammit," Eli swore. Lucas was already past them as he strode forward to meet Caroline, who smiled. Her face was white, but she appeared fine, and Amos Detmer smiled at Lucas. "She's been released," he said as the family gathered around her and she hugged first one and then another of her children.

"Thank God," Eli said, while Lucas turned to Caroline. Ridley Pollard patted her shoulder.

"You're cleared now." Riley turned to shake hands with the other attorney. "Amos, thank you." As the two lawyers talked, Lucas took Caroline's arm.

"Let's get you out of here," Lucas said.

"Seth and I can drive you home," Jillian volunteered.

"You take them home," Eli said. "I'll stay to see about Grant."

"We can stay with Eli," Cole added while Mercedes said she would follow Jillian and Seth to go home with Lucas and Caroline.

One by one, the entire family thanked the lawyers before the men turned to go. Ridley shook hands with Eli. "I'll get back to you. It may be tomorrow before I know whether there will be charges pressed against you or not."

"Thanks, Ridley. I appreciate what you're doing."

"Try to get out of here without taking a swing at anyone," he said, and turned to leave with Amos.

As soon as the family parted, Cole motioned toward the chairs. "This may take hours. We haven't eaten. What about you, Eli?"

"Nope, but I'm not hungry. I'll stay here. You and Dixie go get something. If anything changes, I can call you on your cell."

Cole and Dixie left, and Eli paced the room slowly, finally standing by a window. It was dark outside and streetlights had come on. He was thankful his mother had been released, but he had a growing dread over the lengthening time it was taking for Grant to be questioned. Grant had struck a chord with Eli, who liked him enormously. Grant had that same streak of kindness and generosity that Caroline did. Grant had raised his niece and nephew when their mother had run out on them and his grandparents died. Grant couldn't be the murderer, yet he was a likely suspect.

Eli raked his fingers through his hair and thought about Lara. He was still surprised that she had come to help today. She must care about him to do that. He had to admit that he had fallen in love with her, but a lot of good it would do him. Still, Lara's showing up this afternoon gave him pause about the future.

Cole and Dixie returned with sandwiches, but Eli's appetite had diminished the day he'd met Lara and only grown less since then. He knew from taking his belt in that he was losing weight. Idly, he wondered whether he was losing more sleep or more weight over her. He hardly slept anymore, catching an hour or two and then waking and wanting her.

An hour later Eli paced the floor again. Cole stretched out his long legs and looked at his brother. "Eli, sit down. You'll wear out the floor."

"They're taking too long."

"Yes, they are," Cole answered solemnly. "Ridley thinks Edgar Kent is the best possible lawyer we could get, so at least Grant is in excellent hands."

Eli raked his fingers through his hair and sat down in a chair facing Cole and Dixie. "You two can go if you want, and I'll stay."

"We're fine," Cole said, glancing at Dixie, who nodded. He leaned closer to her, draping his arm around her shoulders. "Tell me if you want to go."

A look passed between them, and Eli was reminded again of Lara. Every time they were together Cole and Dixie's love for each other made Eli feel all the more cold and empty.

It was after nine before Grant and Edgar Kent reappeared. Eli, Dixie and Cole all went forward to him. As soon as Eli introduced Edgar Kent to Dixie and Cole, he turned to Grant. "How'd it go?" Eli asked, knowing from Grant's scowling expression that the answer wouldn't be what he wanted to hear.

Grant's face flushed, and his eyes snapped with anger. "They're not going to hold me here, but I can't leave the area," he announced gruffly. "I'm definitely their prime suspect."

"They don't have any solid evidence to tie you to the crime," Edgar Kent reminded him. "If they want to question you again, just call me first. You know how to get me at any hour, day or night."

Grant turned to the lawyer and extended his hand. "Thanks for being here tonight."

"Glad to do it. I'll see you in my office tomorrow morning," Edgar Kent said and turned to tell the others goodbye.

"I'll take you back with me, and Cole and Dixie can go home," Eli said.

"You didn't do it, Grant. The truth will come out."

"Not if they stop searching for the real killer because they think they've found the murderer in me," Grant said. He held his hand out to Cole. "Thank you and Dixie for coming tonight. It makes me feel better to know that this family supports me. I can't tell all three of you how much that means to me."

"You're part of our family," Eli said. "We'll all stick together. And we know you're innocent."

"The reporters are probably still hanging around in back. Let's get you out the front," Cole said.

"I have to get my car," Eli replied. "I'll make a run for it and meet you—how about in front of St. Mary's Cathedral? You take Grant that far with you, and I'll pick him up there. I can lose any reporters between here and the church."

Cole nodded and the three of them went out the front. Eli strode to the back door, took a deep breath and stepped outside. When he dashed for his car, reporters closed in. Ignoring their questions, he pushed one aside at his car and slid in, locking his doors instantly.

With two cars speeding behind him, Eli raced out of the parking lot and down the street, accelerating up and down hills as he wound through San Francisco. When he decided he had lost everyone on his tail, he headed for Geary Street to pick up Grant.

Keeping an eye on the rearview mirror, Eli's thoughts returned to Lara. He wanted to see her again. The realization that he was in love shocked him, but he had always known what he wanted and now he wanted Lara. It went beyond physical desire. He wanted her in his life, and maybe she was having second thoughts about not seeing him again, too.

He came to a decision about his future.

With clouds of fog hovering over the ground the next morning, Eli drove through the Ashton Estate gate and watched it close behind him. Thanks to Charlotte Ashton, he could get in the private entrance. He thought about his phone conversation with her, setting up a visit to Ashton Estate. He wanted to see Lara and he suspected if he called her, she would refuse.

Eli followed Charlotte's directions and drove around the house to park near the winery. Alexandre said he would be there to pick him up with one of the estate carts and take him to the greenhouse on the east.

Eli stepped out of the car and strode toward the front of the winery where he was to meet Alexandre. Eli knew he would have to do something to show his gratitude to Charlotte and Alexandre for setting up this rendezvous.

Eli remembered meeting Alexandre at a wine tasting event in Yountville, and he had liked the winemaker immediately. They shared a love of wine making, and Eli was impressed with Alexandre's reputation and expertise. Alexandre was obviously deeply in love with Charlotte Ashton, and Eli was glad because he suspected Spencer may have given her a hard time.

As Eli walked, he lifted his face and inhaled. The air smelled damp, but he loved the fog because he knew how great it was for the grapevines. It would also keep him from being seen by anyone in the house. Charlotte had told him that Lilah would be ensconced in the mansion, talking on the telephone to her friends. Trace would be in his office. Walker would not even be at the estate so Eli should be able to safely come and go without interference from the family. Charlotte also promised to get Lara to the greenhouse. Then Eli was on his own.

A twig snapped under his feet. He inhaled again, enjoying the damp air that lifted his spirits in spite of the grayness. The late-morning sun soon would burn off the fog, yet it kept the ground cool and moist in the early part of the day.

Eli's gaze ran over the buildings. He glanced over his shoulder at the magnificent mansion shrouded in fog. Bitterness knotted his stomach. He intended to talk to Mom and Dad again about the will. Spencer shouldn't have inherited it, and Ashton Estate was too much to toss aside with a shrug. Eli knew that part of his motive was revenge against Spencer even though he would never know anyway.

Eli's nerves were raw. He missed Lara more with each passing day, and he prayed that her appearance last night meant she still cared about him.

As he turned a corner, he almost collided with Lilah Ashton.

"You!" she gasped. "What are you doing on our land?" Her eyes widened. To his horror she screamed, a loud, terrified cry that shattered the quiet morning.

Ten

"Trace, help! Trace!"

"Mrs. Ashton," Eli began, intending to explain that he was there to see Alexandre—a story they had decided on earlier if Eli ran into any of the other Ashtons.

Trace burst out of the winery and sprinted toward them. His face was flushed and his fists clenched. "You damn bastard!" he yelled. "Leave my mother alone! I told you to stay away from here."

"You're here to spy on us," Lilah accused. Barely listening to her, Eli braced his feet apart.

"Trace, I'm here—" Eli began, wondering if either mother or son would listen to an explanation.

Trace never slowed. He swung his fist, connecting with Eli's jaw. Eli staggered, and lights danced before his eyes.

His temper snapped and he waded in. His fist shot out in a

right to the jaw. With a crack of bone on bone, Eli sent Trace sprawling.

"Call the police! Call the police!" Lilah Ashton screamed as Trace sprang up to lunge at Eli, tackling him. Both men toppled and rolled across the ground.

"Mrs. Ashton!" Lara cried, running up to join them. Eli heard her voice and wanted to shake Trace off him. He didn't want Lara to take any blame for his being at the estate.

He rolled over on top of Trace, broke away and stood.

"Call the police!" Lilah Ashton still screamed while Lara stood in front of her.

"Ms. Ashton, don't call the police," Lara commanded forcefully enough to startle Lilah Ashton into silence.

"Eli Ashton is here because—" Lara started, but was interrupted by a deep male voice.

Alexandre approached them, stepping between Trace and Eli as Trace got to his feet. Trace's lip was cut while Eli's cheek was bleeding. Both men had smaller cuts. Eli's sleeve was torn, and Trace's shirt was ripped with blood oozing from a scratch on his shoulder.

"Eli Ashton is here to see me," Alexandre announced. "We share a passion for France, and I have maps and pictures for him. Sorry if this caused an upset."

"Next time, Alexandre, tell someone." Trace clamped his jaw closed and turned to stride away.

Frowning, Lilah Ashton blinked and rubbed her forehead. "Very well," she said, turning to hurry after her son. "Trace, wait," she called.

Eli turned to Alexandre. "Thanks for stepping in and saving the situation," he said quietly and offered his hand to Alexandre.

"Glad to. I can take both of you to the greenhouse where you can talk in private."

"That won't be necessary," Lara said. "But thank you, anyway, Alexandre."

He smiled at her, nodded and left them alone.

Taking out his handkerchief to wipe his bleeding cheek, Eli turned to her. "I wanted to see you. Charlotte and Alexandre helped me set up a meeting. Charlotte was going to call you to come to the greenhouse."

"She just did. That's where I was headed when I heard Lilah scream. Then I saw you and Trace. Why didn't you tell me you wanted to see me?"

"I figured you'd refuse."

She frowned at him. "Come with me and we'll wash your cuts."

"I'm all right."

Her fingers closed around his arm. "You come with me," she said, and he fell into step beside her. She led him upstairs to her tiny quarters on the third floor where she closed the door behind them.

Eli glanced around the room that was yellow and white with bright, primary colored pillows and a rocker. Circus prints were hung on one wall and plants were scattered around the room. She had a twin bed that she motioned to.

"Sit there," she said and disappeared back into the hall. He looked around the bedroom/sitting room and thought it was cheerful and cozy and looked like Lara.

She returned to hand him gauze and bandages, antiseptic and a towel. She had a wet washcloth that she dabbed against his cut cheek.

"This is where I live. This floor is for the staff. We have a bathroom down the hall."

"This room looks like you. It's cozy. I like it."

She frowned at him. "It's tiny, Eli," she protested. "You live in that wonderful suite. This is a shoe box."

"It's livable, while the rest of this house looks like a museum—the parlor, the library, the dining room all create a feeling of look, don't touch. Besides, this room is yours, so that makes it special," he said and she shifted her attention to his cut. He noticed that her cheeks were flushed.

Since she was not on duty, she was dressed in a bright-blue cotton shirt and blue cotton slacks and her hair was tied behind her head with a matching blue ribbon. She had sandals on her feet. His mouth went dry as he mentally stripped away the clothes and remembered how she had looked naked in his arms.

In seconds she stood between his legs so she could treat his injured face. When he rested his hands on her hips, she frowned, but then went back to dabbing at the cut on his cheek.

"I think you gave worse than you got," she remarked.

"I grew up wrestling with Cole. Trace only has sisters. He doesn't have my experience," Eli replied dryly. "Walker's enough older than Trace that Trace probably didn't tangle with him much." Eli took a deep breath. "Lara, I want to see you again."

"Eli, you know I can't. I—"

"Charlotte said you're off duty this morning. Is that right?"

She glared at him. "Yes, it is, but that doesn't matter."

"It matters to me," he said, standing and taking her hand. "You're not in uniform, so you must be off duty. Come on. We're going where we can talk."

"I'm not—"

He turned to her. "Lara, please. I want to talk to you," he said in a tone that made Lara's heart melt. As she inhaled deeply, he took her hand and turned to go.

They hurried through the house, and he was glad they didn't encounter any of the Ashtons. At his car he held open the door for her.

"How did you even get through the gate this morning?" Lara asked as she slid into the seat.

"Charlotte and Alexandre," he replied.

Eli strode around the car to sit behind the wheel. "Charlotte saw you leave with me for our family party. You said she was friendly to you and I've met and talked to Alexandre before, so I called Charlotte and told her I wanted to see you. I told her that for the past week, when I've called you, you've simply hung up the phone."

"That's because I've said everything there is to say."

"Charlotte said she would arrange it so I could get in and talk to you at her greenhouse."

"Oh, my word! Charlotte's in love and she sees the whole world in a rosy glow. So what happened?"

"I looked for Alexandre, who agreed to be here this morning to take me to the greenhouse. He said he's finished his work here and they're waiting until Charlotte can go to France with him. Anyway, I ran into Lilah Ashton who, according to Charlotte, would be in the house on the phone."

"She usually is in the mornings. She likes to talk to her friends, she reads the paper and she gives my mom any additional instructions about the staff."

"The minute she saw me, Lilah started screaming for Trace, and he came on the run. As soon as he appeared, we got into it. All the time we fought, Lilah screamed for someone to call the police."

"That's what I heard. I ran out because I thought Lilah was in trouble."

"Even though Trace threw the first punch, I know I shouldn't have hit him. It felt damn satisfying to slug him, though."

"I'm sorry you and Trace fought."

"I'm thankful Alexandre appeared," Eli said. "I wouldn't want you in any trouble because I came to see you."

"This is foolish, Eli," Lara said quietly, and his insides clenched.

He prayed his instincts were right and seeing her wasn't going to be another rejection.

"I want to go where we can be alone and talk. I have things I need to tell you," he said as he sped toward Napa. "I've missed seeing you. It meant a lot to my family that you were there for Mom and Grant last night."

"I was glad to be present. What happened with Grant?"

"At this point it looks as if he is a prime suspect."

"Oh, no!" she gasped. "That's terrible!"

"They didn't arrest him, because they don't have enough hard evidence, but they told him he can't leave the area."

"That's awful and I know it upsets your family!" Lara exclaimed.

"We're worried that the police will stop searching for the murderer. They've been under pressure to solve the crime. The press is wild to get news about the scandalous Ashtons and the murder. Meanwhile, our whole family believes in Grant's innocence. That man could no more have done such a deed than Dad could have."

"You said Grant doesn't have an alibi and he has a motive."

"There has to be more than that to take him to court. In the meantime, he's on edge about the situation. The family, including Anna and little Jack, try to cheer him."

"He's fortunate to have all of you."

"We're glad to have him in the family. For such a rotten man, Spencer fathered some likable people."

"I saw you on the news last night, and your picture is in the paper this morning."

He groaned. "I figured. I didn't look at the paper today and I didn't watch the news last night, but I'm not surprised. I haven't talked to our lawyer yet about it, but he's trying to keep me out of jail."

"Don't even say that!" she exclaimed.

Eli glanced at her, longing to touch her and wishing he could pull her close against his side. "I'm going to look at apartments in Napa."

"Why?" she asked.

He shrugged. "I thought I might want to be off on my own this coming year. I can stay at the house whenever I want. That's what Mercedes does all the time."

As they talked, he drove into Napa and headed to the restaurant and hotel where he and Lara spent their first night together. When he parked and got out to open her door, she looked up at him.

"What are we doing here?"

"I told you. I want to talk to you alone. Come on. We'll just talk and then I'll take you to lunch.

He took her hand to enter the hotel, and Lara's pulse raced. She should say no firmly and insist they talk somewhere less private, but Eli had a determined look in his eye and a steely note in his voice. And she had missed him beyond belief.

She watched him cross the hotel lobby to the desk. Looking sexy and adorable, he wore navy slacks and a navy knit shirt that now had a rip in the sleeve. In spite of the cuts and bruises and the rip in his clothes, he was incredibly appealing.

She had hurt terribly for him and for his family yesterday when she'd heard the news on the radio. She'd felt compelled to go see if she could help them in San Francisco.

Memories of their first night assailed her, and she grew hot just thinking about that night. Then he was striding back to her, his scalding gaze consuming her and making her heart pound.

"Let's go," he said, taking her hand. Upstairs, they had the same suite, and she wondered if he had made arrangements ahead of time but then decided he hadn't. She suspected her appearance last night had triggered his visit today.

He unlocked the door of the suite and held it open for her. She entered and turned to face him, trying to summon the strength and resistance she knew she was going to desperately need.

"All right, Eli. We're alone and we can talk, but it won't change anything."

"I hope it will change everything," he said in a husky voice, closing and locking the door and then turning to face her. He stepped to her to catch both of her hands in his.

"Lara, I know I'm hot-tempered and I know I like to be in control. Maybe way too much of both of those. I know I'm not worthy of your love because of—"

"Eli," she said, interrupting him, hurting for him and wanting him. "That isn't why I don't want to see you. You're worthy of my love, of any woman's love!"

He dropped her hands to frame her face with his hands. When he stepped closer and gazed down into her eyes, her heart thudded so loudly she was certain he could hear it. Standing this close, she couldn't keep from looking at his mouth, his full underlip, and remembering his kisses. She wanted to kiss him, but she fought the temptation.

"Lara, I've missed you and don't want to be without you," he said in a husky voice.

Lara's pounding heart missed a beat as she gazed up at him. "Eli, I have plans—"

"Shh," he said without letting her finish. "Listen to me. I want you in my life. Adjust your goals and make room for me. If we're married, you can still go to law school."

"Married!" she exclaimed, her eyes widening, shocked by his statement. "We haven't even talked about being in love."

"I guess it took our separation to make me realize the depth of my feelings. I've been miserable. I've missed you every second. I see you everywhere. I can't eat or sleep or even work efficiently. My vineyards that I used to love so much no longer hold my interest. I love you. I know what I want, Lara. I want to marry you."

Stunned at the depth of his feelings for her, she gazed up at him while her heart thudded. Everything in her cried out, yes! She'd known she loved him. Yet she knew the responsibilities she had in her future. Trembling, she ached to reach for him, to kiss him and toss aside all other considerations. This tall, strong man was the love of her life, and she knew there would never be another like him for her. Hurt and sadness and hot desire warred in her while she tingled all over.

"Eli," she said woodenly, "I want to take care—"

"You want to take care of your mother. Lara, don't you think that I, of all people, can understand your need to care for her?" His eyes blazed. "From the time I was eight years old until I was twenty-one and Louret was successfully established I wanted to do all I could to make my mother's life easier. Even when Mom married Lucas, I still wanted that. My goal of making Louret successful was for her sake. That's all I ever wanted. If you marry me, we can both take care of your mother."

Stunned, Lara stared at him. Never had she imagined that he would make her such an offer. "Eli, I don't know what to say…"

"Just say yes that you'll marry me, and I'll take care of the rest," he said, his gaze searching hers. "Lara, will you marry me?"

The words hung in the air like golden baubles dangled before her, promising undreamed-of delights. Marry him! All her reservations fell away. He had promised law school and that together they would take care of her mother. The moment those concerns were resolved, Lara let out a long breath and threw her arms around his neck.

"I love you, Eli!" she exclaimed, and then kissed him before he could reply.

Her mouth covered his, her tongue seeking his to stroke and taste while he kissed her in return. Her insides clenched, and heat started low in her belly. She wanted him with all the pent-up desire that she had battled since that first night. They were so close she could feel his hard erection.

Eli shifted away a few inches to allow him access to her clothing. His fingers twisted free the buttons on her blue blouse to pull it off her shoulders. In minutes he whisked away her blue slacks. "I love you, Lara, and I want you. Heart and soul and body—I want you. I want to kiss and lick every inch of your body," he whispered in her ear, his warm breath tickling her. "I've waited and dreamed of this moment." His husky voice was a mere rasp.

As he pushed her away, she tugged his shirt free, seeing the bulge in his slacks that proclaimed his readiness for her. The moment his strong, muscled chest was bare, she ran her fingers over him, touching his flat nipples and brushing her fingers over his chest hair, then letting her hand drift down to unbuckle his belt.

While she removed his slacks, he kicked off his loafers and peeled away his socks.

"You're so handsome," she declared, running her hands over his bare hips and relishing the male perfection of him. He loved her! It was magic to know. They would marry! Her heart pounded with joy and desire. She slid her hands down to his strong thighs.

"How I love you!" she exclaimed.

While she caressed his legs and teased her fingers up and over his flat stomach, he cupped her breasts, flicking loose the fastener and pushing away her lacy bra.

"Ahh, perfect," he said, palming each soft breast in his big hands. His rough, callused fingers were a sexy abrasion to her tender skin. As his thumbs circled her nipples with deliberation, she gasped and closed her eyes. Clinging to his strong arms, she wallowed in sensations that set her ablaze.

"Eli," she whispered.

"Do you like this?" he asked as he caressed her nipples. He leaned down to take one in his mouth and slowly circle the taut bud with his tongue. Warm and wet, each stroke of his tongue heightened her need until she shook. She slid her hands down, closing her fingers around his smooth, thick shaft. Then she let her tongue circle one of his nipples before she knelt in front of him.

Her tongue lazed down across his flat belly while she let her warm breath sigh over him, her tongue flicking around his shaft, tormenting him until he groaned. Then when she licked his long, throbbing rod, he wound his fingers in her hair.

"Lara!" he rasped, while she slipped one hand down between

his legs to cup him and stroke him. She curled her tongue around the velvet tip of his thick shaft. He shook, and the fingers of his left hand bit into her shoulder.

With a groan he bent down to pull her to her feet. He stopped and removed a packet from his trousers and then he scooped her into his arms to place her on the bed. He tossed the packet on the bedside table. Eli caught her ankles to pull her to the edge of the bed, kneeling between her legs to gently bite and tease along the inside of her thigh.

Lara's heart pounded and she combed her fingers through his hair. She wanted him inside her. She ached, all the longing she had lived with through lonely nights compounding the desire she had now.

"I want to make you come again and again," he whispered while his lips and tongue brushed her inner thigh. She raised her head to find him watching her. He spread her legs, moving between them, parting her soft folds to stroke her with his tongue.

"Eli!" she gasped, closing her eyes while she clung to his strong shoulders. He pushed her back on the bed, lifting her legs over his shoulders and then his tongue licked her intimately. She moved her hips, spreading her legs wider. She was open, utterly his.

"Eli, I want you."

"I'm going to love you until you come apart in my arms," he whispered, holding her legs wider and exploring her with his tongue. Hot and wet, each touch increased the urgency that was coiling in her.

She moved, lost now to his loving. He lifted her hips, giving him more access and then she felt his finger enter her, another torment that pushed her closer to a brink. She spasmed over the edge, her hips shifting in a pounding rhythm while she held him.

"Eli!" she cried in ecstasy. The world vanished except for the sexy man loving her. "Come here. I want you in me."

"Later," he said. "I want to make love to you for hours, Lara," he whispered. He lay down beside her, his hand going where his mouth had been while he propped himself up and leaned down to kiss her breast.

Now his fingers stroked her, an erotic friction that created a stronger need than before. She sat up to nuzzle his neck, teasing him, taking his shaft in her hand to stroke him, but then as his fingers rubbed between her soft folds, she gasped and squeezed her eyes shut, her hips moving again, seeking release and lost to his touch.

"I want you!" she cried.

"I need you to want me," he whispered. "I want to do everything I can for you, to make you climax again and again. When you're excited, it excites me," he said against her throat.

She barely heard him for her pounding pulse. Urgency drove her as she spiraled out of control.

"Eli!" she cried, winding her arm around his neck and pressing him into the bed. She stretched on his naked body, feeling his erection pulse between them while she kissed him hard on the mouth. His hands played over her bottom and slid down between her legs.

Consumed by desire, Lara straddled him and grasped his thick rod.

He shifted and picked her up in his arms, his body warm and naked against hers. "Not yet, babe. Later when I've loved you senseless."

He sat on the edge of the bed and turned her, settling her on his lap. His legs wrapped around hers. He spread their legs wide while his hand played with her nipple and his other hand went between her thighs. "Look, Lara. I love to look at your body, and I've dreamed about you every night since that first night," he said. "Look at us," he commanded.

She opened her eyes and gazed across the room at the mirrored wall. She saw their reflections, her skin pale against Eli's dark body, his strong, tanned arm around her and his hand cupping her breast while his thumb played over her nipple. Their legs were entwined and his fingers moved on her intimately, stirring tension again. She blushed and then gasped and closed her eyes as he drove her to move her hips faster.

"I want you!" she exclaimed. "I can't keep on. I want you now!"

He kissed her ear, his tongue tracing the delicate curve while his fingers continued the sensual magic that was taking her into a raging fire.

When she was on another brink, he released her, turning her to cradle her against his chest and kiss her. Wanting him, loving him with all her being, Lara knew her heart was already his. Ablaze with carnal need, she pushed him down, sprinkling kisses over him and then sliding to the floor to kneel between his legs while her tongue traced along his inner thigh on first one leg and then the other. She pushed him back on the bed with her hand and flicked her tongue over him, taking his shaft in her mouth to lick and suck.

Eli groaned, sliding off the bed to the floor where he pulled her into his arms to kiss her. She clung to him, kissing him passionately in return, rubbing against him and wanting him desperately. He reached out to grab the packet from the bedside table.

Standing, he picked her up, placing her on the bed and moving between her legs. He watched her, his green-eyed gaze as stormy as a windswept sea while he put on the condom.

She drank in the sight of him, ready to love, aroused and hot, the man she would love forever. He came down between her legs, sliding an arm beneath her to hold her while he pushed into her slightly and then withdrew.

She cried out, clutching his bottom and pulling him to her, locking her long legs around him. "Love me!" she demanded hoarsely.

"We're taking our time. Slow, hot loving to drive you wild," he said and kissed her ear while his shaft entered her again before he withdrew. She arched beneath him, her hands raking over his firm buttocks again to pull him close.

"You want it, don't you?" he whispered in her ear. "I want to drive you wild."

She held him tightly with her legs wrapped around him while the exquisite torment created a heart-pounding craving.

"Love me, Eli! Love me now," she cried, raking her fingers down his smooth back and squeezing his buttocks.

He bit her throat lightly while he moved slowly, thrusting and withdrawing. His forehead was beaded with sweat. She thrashed beneath him, urging him to give her more until he lost his iron control. His hips thrust in a primeval rhythm that set off fireworks in her. Lights exploded behind her closed lids and sensations racked her as her urgency grew.

While release sent tremors coursing through her body, she held him tightly. She knew he'd climaxed when his strong body shuddered. His weight settled on her. This was Eli in her arms, Eli loving her, Eli one with her, Eli wanting to marry her!

"I love you, Lara," he said solemnly, and raised his head to rain feathery kisses from her temple to her mouth where he lingered with a thorough kiss.

Sated, Eli rolled to his side and propped his head on his hand to look at her while he drew his fingers languorously down from her throat to her breast, then across her stomach and lower to her thigh. His heart pounded with happiness and he wanted to trail kisses all over her.

"You're beautiful. And perfect. Creamy and pink and auburn hair. I've dreamed about you and wanted you. And I wanted to drive you wild with loving, to make you want me.

She raked locks of his short hair off his forehead. "I couldn't possibly want you more than I do. You do drive me wild. I'm exhausted. I can't stand on my own two feet," she remarked as her fingers traced his jaw. "You're getting a black eye."

"It was worth getting to slug Trace."

She sighed. "I've fallen in love with a fiery, strong-willed, incredibly sexy man who has my heart completely. I'm mush with you."

"Delicious mush," he murmured as he nuzzled her throat. Happiness filled him to the point he couldn't stop smiling at her. "You're as necessary to my life now as those vineyards I love. I love you with all my being, and I want to spend a lifetime making you happy and taking care of you."

She sighed and curled her arm around his neck to kiss him. When he raised his head, he showered light kisses on her temple.

"I worried about my temper," he said, trying to put worries into words. "My family thinks I'm hotheaded and I guess I am. I hate to admit it, but I know where I get my hot temper."

"You'd never vent it against someone you love. I'll bet you've never lost your temper with your mother," she said.

He shook his head. "No, I haven't. And not with Dad or Jillian, either. Mercedes and I have had some hot arguments. Cole and I have our moments."

"That's sibling rivalry, I'd imagine, although I don't know much about brother-sister relationships. I don't think you'd ever really hurt anyone you love."

He grinned. "In the past, Cole and I have gotten plenty physical."

"I love it when you smile, Eli," she said. "You don't smile very often. You're so earnest about life."

"I've had a lot of reasons to be. I've had hell in my life and I've been to the point of giving up on everyone."

"Not anymore," she said, rolling over to smile at him. "You're a good man."

Eli inhaled deeply. "I'm the luckiest man on earth now," he said. "I have you and that's the best."

"You're ridiculous," she exclaimed, laughing with a sparkle in her eyes.

"When can we marry? Make it as soon as possible, Lara."

She rubbed her forehead and gazed into space. "My mother has cousins who live back east. I'll be in law school, too, which means I'll need more time to plan. With Spencer's murder unsolved and everyone in a turmoil, I think we should have a small, quiet wedding. And if we'll wait a bit, maybe they'll have Spencer's murder solved and that won't be in everyone's thoughts constantly."

"Whatever you want, love," Eli murmured, running his tongue in circles on her breast.

"Eli!" she gasped and caught his head to frame his face with her hands. "I can't think about anything when you do that."

"Is that so?" he asked, amused. "All right. You need some time to plan our wedding, so what month are we talking about? October?"

"I was thinking more like January."

He groaned. "That's incredibly long. How about November?" he asked as if he were bidding at auction. He played with silky locks of her hair.

"I'd like December. Then we can have a Christmas wedding," she exclaimed with enthusiasm. "I'd like that. Now, are you going to give me a hard time about this?"

"December it is. Let's find an apartment right away and move into it." He gazed into her light-brown eyes and wanted her as if they hadn't just made love for a couple of hours. "Will you?" he asked and when she nodded, he smiled. "I'm the happiest winemaker in the whole wide world."

She laughed and nuzzled his neck. He tightened his arm around her tiny waist and relished her softness and naked body against him. "We need to tell the family and your mother. The other Ashtons can go to hell."

Lara sat up and shook her head. "No, they can't," she said solemnly. "I've grown up with them. You may not like them, and I know there's bitterness between you and Trace—"

"And Walker and Lilah Ashton," he interjected, running his hands across Lara's breasts and watching her nipples tighten. She inhaled and caught up the sheet to hold it in front of her.

"Listen to me, Eli. I've known them forever. Paige and Megan are fine people. So is Simon Pearce, Megan's husband. Charlotte has been wonderful, and I like Alexandre."

"I wasn't talking about Charlotte and Alexandre."

"I know. You were thinking about Trace and Walker. I want all of them at our wedding. Trace and Walker are fine people, too. They're not like Spencer. Trace isn't at all."

He stared at her, seeing a stubborn tilt to her chin. "Are we having our first fight?"

"I don't know. Are we?"

Suddenly he gave her a crooked smile. "Ask the whole rotten family if you want to. Even Trace. He won't attend my wedding, you know."

She hugged Eli and laughed. "He'll attend mine. They're not rotten. Stop letting Spencer influence your feelings," she said suddenly, sitting up to gaze at him solemnly.

Eli played with her hair and shook his head. "I don't think I can. But for you, I'll give it a try."

"I'm going to make you so happy you won't think about Spencer or your anger at Trace. Or always being in control," she exclaimed, leaning down to tease his nipple with her tongue.

He laughed, treasuring her softness, loving her kisses and knowing his life was changing for the better forever. He rolled her over to lie on top of her and gaze into her warm brown eyes. "From this day forward, my life will be better than ever before," he admitted to her. "Happier, sexier, more fulfilled. How I love you! Let's go tell our families. Maybe we'll all go to dinner tonight and celebrate. We can ask Charlotte and Alexandre to join us."

"That would be wonderful!" Lara exclaimed, her eyes shining.

"I want to ask the Nebraska Ashtons. We can call Russ and Abigail now."

"I don't know them," Lara said.

"Russ was foreman for our vineyards. Russ's dad was Lucas's best friend and when he and Russ's mother were killed—"

"Let me guess. Lucas and Caroline took Russ in."

"Of course. Russ was my right-hand man—he was fantastic with the vineyards and I miss him like hell. Abigail was raised by Grant, who's her uncle. I want Russ and Abigail to know about our engagement. And we have to call my younger brother, Mason, who is a winemaker and studying in France."

"Doesn't Grant have a nephew, too?"

"Yes and we'll invite him to the wedding. I think he and Grant are close. I think Grant's sister, Grace, is the one who is like Spencer. She abandoned her two kids, and eventually Grant ended up raising them."

"Where is Grace?"

"No one knows. At least not as far as I know. Grant sure as hell doesn't and neither does Abigail. That's Spencer all over again. I don't want to think about Spencer today." He brushed a kiss across Lara's lips. "I'll reserve this suite for the rest of the week. For now, let's drive into San Francisco and get you an engagement ring."

"Just like that?"

"Just like that," he answered. "We'll find something you like."

Her laugh was smothered by his kiss.

Epilogue

The last night of June, music and laughter wafted from the terrace of The Vines. Lanterns shed soft light on an engagement party that Lucas and Caroline were holding for Eli and Lara.

Eli moved out of a circle of friends and searched for Lara. He'd gotten separated from her earlier. He saw Grant talking to Charlotte and Alexandre. Eli worried about Grant, wanting the police to find the real murderer, because the press was hounding Grant and printing stories about his life in Nebraska, focusing on him as if he were Spencer's killer.

He found Lara in a group with Franci, Anna, Jillian and Seth and two of Jillian's friends. The women were admiring the three-carat emerald-cut engagement ring he'd bought her the very day he'd asked her to marry him. Jack had already been tucked into bed and a sitter was with him so Anna could attend the party. For a moment Eli feasted on the sight of his fiancée who looked ravishing in a sleeveless yellow dress. She wore the necklace he had given her and no other jewelry except his ring. With his pulse racing, Eli took Lara's arm.

"Excuse us," he said. As soon as he pulled her aside, he placed his hands on her shoulders. "I've partied long enough. I want to get you to myself and make wild, passionate love with you."

She smiled at him and stroked his arm. "Sounds super to me except we're the guests of honor so I think we're supposed to stay until the last of the company leaves."

Eli groaned. "I was afraid you'd say that."

"I'm not going to have your family think I don't know what's proper. Just hang on to your coattails and wait a little longer. Jillian said she and Seth are leaving soon. Mercedes and Craig Bradford have already gone. I think the party will break up in the next hour. Anna is leaving any minute now to relieve the sitter. It'll be over soon."

"Can I show you my etchings in my suite?" he asked, and she laughed.

"No, you can't! Not now. Just be polite and enjoy the evening. I'm having a wonderful time, and I love your family."

"Good. I love them, too. And your mom is a character. I'm getting to know her better."

"Charlotte and Alexandre asked her to ride over with them. Speaking of them, did Alexandre tell you that he and Charlotte get to leave the country?"

"Alexandre told me. I'm glad, except I think it's at Grant's expense because all suspicion has been turned on him."

"You're right. The police have told Charlotte that she can go, so she and Alexandre leave in three days. The police suspected her at first because she's the one who found Spencer's body."

"I'm glad she's cleared, but I worry about Grant. I hope he's cleared soon. I think Anna worries about him as much as our family does. Of course, she and Jack are part of our family now, anyway."

Cole and Dixie approached. "We're leaving," Cole said. "Congratulations again, we're happy for both of you. Lara, you're going to have to be patient to put up with my brother."

She laughed. "I think I can manage," she said, as Eli slipped his arm around her waist.

"He's joking," Dixie said, giving Cole a gentle poke with her forefinger. "It's been a great party."

"We've got to find Mom and Dad," Cole said.

Eli pointed. "There's Dad, talking to Grant."

Within the hour the party broke up. The only ones left were Caroline and Lucas.

"Thank you so much for the delightful party," Lara said.

"We're glad to have you as part of the family now," Caroline said.

"It's been great," Eli said, brushing a kiss on his mother's cheek. "Thanks, both of you." Lucas clasped Eli on the shoulder.

"I'm happy for you and Lara," Lucas said. He looked at Lara. "You're a great influence on him."

"I hope so," she said, smiling at his parents.

"We'll see you tomorrow," Eli said, putting his arm around Lara's shoulders to lead her away.

He drove to Napa and pulled into the garage of a tall, Victorian that Lara loved.

"Eli, I still can't believe you bought this house. You were going to get an apartment."

"Don't you like our house?"

"I adore it. I feel like Cinderella with you."

He laughed. "I can't quite see myself as Prince Charming. And you as Cinderella—no."

"I had an ordinary, routine, rather drab life until you swept me out of it."

"That describes me and my life," he said.

"Hardly! And this house is fantastic. More than I ever dreamed I would live in."

"It's great because you're here with me," he replied. "We can stay in my suite when we want to be at Louret. In the meantime, we have this house, and it's close enough. We'll find a house here in town for your mom. Lara, I meant it. Your mom can quit her job right now if she wants to."

"I've talked to her about it," Lara said as they walked beneath a trellis covered by yellow roses. They crossed the wraparound porch, and Eli unlocked the back door, holding it for Lara to enter.

"She wants to work until the wedding in December. By then we'll have a house here for her and she can quit."

Eli pulled Lara into his arms. A soft light burned over the counter across the kitchen from them, and she wrapped her arms around Eli's waist, looking up at her adorable fiancé. "I love you with all my heart, Eli."

"It's so great. You've made me the happiest man on this earth," he replied, and then his mouth covered hers, taking her answer. He leaned over her, tightening his arms around her while he kissed her.

Lara stood on tiptoe, pressing against her strong hero while her heart pounded with excitement and joy. She knew she was the happiest bride-to-be on earth. She loved Eli with all her being and knew she would all her life.

* * * * *

DYNASTIES:THE ASHTONS
continues next month with
Sheri WhiteFeather's
BETRAYED BIRTHRIGHT!

Welcome to Silhouette Desire's brand-new installment of

*The drama unfolds for six of
the state's wealthiest bachelors.*

BLACK-TIE SEDUCTION
by Cindy Gerard
(Silhouette Desire #1665, July 2005)

LESS-THAN-INNOCENT INVITATION
by Shirley Rogers
(Silhouette Desire #1671, August 2005)

STRICTLY CONFIDENTIAL ATTRACTION
by Brenda Jackson
(Silhouette Desire #1677, September 2005)

*Look for three more titles from Michelle Celmer,
Sara Orwig and Kristi Gold to follow.*

COMING NEXT MONTH

#1663 BETRAYED BIRTHRIGHT—Sheri WhiteFeather
Dynasties: The Ashtons
When Walker Ashton decided to search for his past, he found it on a
Sioux Nation reservation. Helping him to deal with his Native American
heritage was Tamra Winter Hawk, a woman who cherished her roots
and had Walker longing for a future together. But when his real-world
commitments intruded upon their fantasy liaison, would they find a way
to keep the connection they'd formed?

#1664 THE LAST REILLY STANDING—Maureen Child
Three-Way Wager
Aidan Reilly was determined to win the bet he'd made with his brothers.
Three months without sex meant one thing: spend *a lot* of time with his
best gal pal, Terry Evans. She had given up on love long ago because the
pain just wasn't worth it. Then…temptation proved to be too much. The last
Reilly standing had lost the bet, but could he win the girl?

#1665 BLACK-TIE SEDUCTION—Cindy Gerard
Texas Cattleman's Club: The Secret Diary
Millionaire Jacob Thorne got on Christine Travers's last nerve—the sensible
lady had no time for Jacob's flirtatious demeanor. But when the two butted
heads at an auction, Jacob embarked on a black-tie seduction that would
prove she had needs—womanly needs—that only he could satisfy.

#1666 THE RUGGED LONER—Bronwyn Jameson
Princes of the Outback
Australian widower Tomas Carlisle was stunned to learn he had to father
a child to inherit a cattle empire. Making a deal with longtime friend
Angelina Mori seemed the perfect solution—until their passion escalated
and Angelina mounted an all-out attack on Tomas's defense against hot,
passionate, *committed* love.

#1667 CRAVING BEAUTY—Nalini Singh
They'd married within mere days of meeting. Successful tycoon
Marc Bordeaux had been enchanted by Hira Dazirah's desert beauty. But
Hira feared Marc only craved her outer good looks. This forced Marc to
prove his true feelings to his virgin bride—and tender actions spoke louder
than words.…

#1668 LIKE LIGHTNING—Charlene Sands
Although veterinarian Maddie Brooks convinced rancher Trey Walker to
allow her to live and work on his ranch, there was no way Trey would ever
romance the sweet and sexy Maddie. He was a victim of the "Walker Curse"
and couldn't commit to any woman. But once they gave in to temptation,
Maddie was determined to make their arrangement more permanent.…

SDCNM0605

presents

the final installment of

THREE WAY WAGER

*The Reilly triplets bet they could go
ninety days without sex. Hmm.*

THE LAST
REILLY STANDING

by Maureen Child

(SD #1664, available July 2005)

Aidan Reilly was determined to win the bet
he'd made with his brothers. Three months
without sex meant one thing: spend *a lot* of
time with his best gal pal Terry Evans. She had
given up on love long ago because the pain
just wasn't worth it. Then…temptation proved
to be too much. The last Reilly standing had
lost the bet, but could he win the girl?

Available at your favorite retail outlet.